#4

Cup Crazy

Gordon Korman

AN
APPLE
PAPERBACK

SCHOLASTIC INC.

New York Toronto London Auckland Sydney
Mexico City New Delhi Hong Kong

For Brandon Pekilis,
a fellow hockey fan

No part of this publication may be reproduced in whole or in part, or stored in a retrieval system, or transmitted in any form or by any means, electronic, mechanical, photocopying, recording, or otherwise, without written permission of the publisher. For information regarding permission, write to Scholastic Inc., Attention: Permissions Department, 555 Broadway, New York, NY 10012.

ISBN 0-590-70630-6

12 11 10 9 8 7 6 5 4 3 2 1   0 1 2 3 4 5 6/0

Printed in the U.S.A.   40

First Scholastic printing, April 2000

||||| _Chapter 1_

Playoffs.

No word brings out more excitement in a hockey fan. The long grueling regular season is over. Most of the teams didn't measure up, and they're gone, talking about "what if" and "next year." And who's left? The best of the best, ready to do battle for the ultimate prize — the championship.

Sports Illustrated has done more cover stories on playoffs than on any other subject. That's where I come in. Chipmunk Adelman, sports reporter. (Please don't call me by my real name — Clarence.)

To be honest, I don't work for _Sports Illustrated_ just yet. But in the Waterloo Elementary School _Gazette_, hockey is my beat.

That's why I was riding to the big playoff meeting on the team bus of the Mars Health Food Stars.

There I sat, on a fifty-pound bag of oat bran, interviewing the players at this big moment.

"How does it feel to make the playoffs in your very first year?" I asked, clicking on my mini-tape recorder.

"It's a miracle that we got into the league at all!" chortled Josh Colwin, the goalie, who was perched on a barrel of tofu. "Making the playoffs is like winning the lottery!"

I should explain about the tofu, oat bran, bean sprouts, soy meal, and carob gum piled all around us. This "bus" was actually the delivery van for Mars Health Food, the team sponsor. Boom Boom Bolitsky, the owner, was also the Stars' coach.

Coach Bolitsky was a retired NHL player from the 1970s. Don't worry if you've never heard of him. Nobody has. He was a last-round draft choice who spent most of his career being traded and sent down to the minors. But hey — he played in the NHL. That was more than you could say for any other coach in the Waterloo Slapshot League. You bet we were proud of him!

We pulled into the parking lot of the community center, and Coach Bolitsky opened the cargo doors of the van. He grinned at us, revealing his three missing teeth — remember, hockey players didn't wear face guards in the 1970s.

"Okay," he said, "everybody out of the whatcha-macallit."

We all climbed down and gathered around him on the pavement.

"Are you whosises ready to find out who we play in the first round of the doohickeys?"

That was another thing about Boom Boom. It wasn't so easy to understand what he was talking about. When he couldn't come up with the name of something, he'd substitute words like *thingamajig*, *whatchamacallit*, *dingus*, *heejazz*, and *gizmo*. When you got to know him, you kind of learned to translate a little. For example, "the first round of doohickeys" just meant "the first round of playoffs." But sometimes he'd blurt out something like, "Put the thinga-mawhosis in the whatchamagizmo." I'm still trying to figure that one out.

We gave the coach a big cheer and followed him into the building.

The community center housed the ice rink, but tonight we were headed for the auditorium. It was time for the big drawing that would determine the matchups for the eight playoff teams.

The room was crowded with players, parents, and league officials. A buzz arose when Boom Boom led us inside.

There were a number of reasons for this. For

starters, our coach wasn't the handsomest guy in town. I know beauty is only skin deep. But Boom Boom resembled a six-foot praying mantis, complete with bulging eyes and bent-over posture. He was totally bald in front, but the back of his head sported a bushy ponytail that stood straight out when he got excited.

But the crowd was also murmuring about Alexia Colwin, Josh's twin sister. Alexia was the Stars' captain, and the only girl ever to play in the Slapshot League. I don't think the other teams were thrilled to have to skate against a girl. But what really freaked them out was how good she was. Alexia was the real deal — strong, tough, and by far the best checker in the league. She was also number nine on the scoring list. It would be hard to find a better two-way player.

As we stood there, some wise guy called out, "The Martians are here!"

We all groaned. That was the main reason why we created such a stir with this crowd. You see, we played in the Waterloo League, went to Waterloo schools, and used their library and police department and all that. But we weren't from Waterloo. Our town, Mars, was barely two miles away across a canal that was thirty feet wide at its broadest point. It was nothing, right? We were all neighbors, one big happy family?

Forget it. They looked down on us, made fun of us, called us Martians and space hicks and nebula nerds. It had taken *thirty years* for the Waterloo Slap-shot League to run out of excuses why we Marsers couldn't have a team. That's how come it felt so good to be in the playoffs. Those Waterloo types had expected us to wash out after the first month.

"Hey, guys! Over here!"

Trent Ruben had his coat, his gloves, his scarf, his sweater, and one shoe spread out all over the front row, saving seats for us. He was our assistant captain, and the only Waterloo kid on the Stars. Man, were we lucky to get him! He was the league's leading scorer and a really great guy.

We scrambled to our chairs and high-fived our Waterloo teammate.

Trent slapped me on the back. "Ready for the playoffs, Chipmunk?"

That's why I loved the Stars from Mars. Even though I wasn't a player, they treated me like one of them. I was the team reporter. No other team had one. Not even the first-place Penguins.

"Ready?" I repeated. "I'm psyched! I just spent twenty-five dollars on spare batteries!"

"Well, what do you know?" came a voice from behind us. "A flock of Martians!"

I didn't have to turn around to know who it was.

Happer Feldman of the Penguins. His friend and line mate, Oliver Witt, was with him as usual.

"I didn't know the playoffs had gone interplanetary," sneered Oliver.

The whole front row started shaking. I knew what that was. Here we were, trying to give those two idiots the silent treatment, and our winger Cal Torelli was laughing at their rotten jokes. It wasn't Cal's fault. He laughs at everything.

"Oh, look, the astro-geek has a sense of humor!" exclaimed Happer.

I thought Cal was going to bust a gut.

"Shut up, stupid," whispered Jared Enoch, another of our wingers.

Oliver reached out to yank Alexia's long hair. But before his hand was halfway there, she said in a low voice — without turning around — "Don't even think about it."

He pulled away his hand like it had been burned.

That was classic Alexia. The quieter she said something, the louder her message got through. She whispered what the rest of us would be yelling. I call it reverse volume control.

Suddenly, there were oohs and aahs in the auditorium. Onstage, the league officials were hoisting the championship trophy, the gleaming Feldman Cup. It was named after Happer's grandfather, who was the founder of the Waterloo Slapshot League. The current president was also a Feldman — Happer's uncle. And since Happer was on the Penguins, a Feldman was probably going to win the championship this year.

"The league president is holding up the greatest prize in Slapshot hockey," I murmured into my tape recorder.

Happer pinched my neck. "Put your eyes back in your head, Chipmunk. No Martian is ever going to lay an alien finger on that trophy."

Alexia's reverse volume control drifted over her shoulder once more. "Don't make promises you can't keep, bigmouth."

But Happer was smug. "Oh, this one's guaranteed. You'll find out."

Chapter 2 \|\|\|\|\|

My reporter's sense tingled. What did he mean by that?

But my attention soon shifted to the drama on the stage. The names of the eight playoff teams were placed in the Feldman Cup. Then the draw began.

"The Ferguson Ford Flames will be playing the Powerhouse Gas and Electric Penguins."

Sighs of relief were heard around the room. Everyone knew that a first-round matchup with the Penguins was a sure ticket to an early summer. There were some groans, too, mostly from the Flames.

The Stars drew the Baker's Auto Body Bruins. They beat us pretty badly this year, 6–2. But that was way back in the beginning of the season. The Stars really hadn't had a chance to click at that early point.

I dictated a headline idea into my tape recorder. "*A Shot at Revenge.*"

"The Bruins are tough," Trent whispered, "but I think we can take them."

"Let's see how confident you are ten minutes from now," snickered Happer.

Oh, I didn't like the sound of that. Something was up. I could smell it.

After the drawing was finished, we stood around the big chart and tried to map out how we thought the playoffs would go:

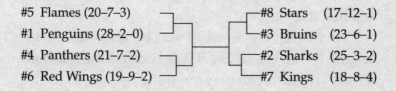

#5 Flames (20–7–3)
#1 Penguins (28–2–0)
#4 Panthers (21–7–2)
#6 Red Wings (19–9–2)

#8 Stars   (17–12–1)
#3 Bruins   (23–6–1)
#2 Sharks   (25–3–2)
#7 Kings   (18–8–4)

"If we get past the Bruins," Josh mused, "then we play the winner of the Sharks against the Kings."

"So long as it's not the Penguins," breathed Jared.

Everyone nodded in agreement. If we had to face the mighty Powerhouse Gas and Electric, it wouldn't be until the final round. That was the way the matchups laid out.

I'll bet we could have stood there all night, figuring the angles while the place emptied out.

Boom Boom grew a little impatient with us. "All

right, zip up your whatsits. It's time to get out to the heejazz." *Zip up your coats. It's time to get out to the truck.*

"Hold on there, Bolitsky. I need a word with you and your team."

It was Mr. Feldman. Uh-oh. Happer's uncle was one of those guys who had voted against letting Mars have a team in the Slapshot League. If he had something to say, it was probably bad news.

"Bolitsky," began the league president, "we're all really happy to have Alexia Colwin as your captain. And no one is more proud of what she's accomplished than me."

Don't believe a word of it. The only reason the league let her on the Stars was because the Supreme Court says girls can play anything they want.

Mr. Feldman went on. "But it has come to my attention that it's illegal to have her in the league."

I was so shocked I was tongue-tied. The players were too. But not Boom Boom.

"That's a load of whatchamacallit!" he exclaimed.

"Garbage," Alexia translated quietly.

"I'm just as upset as you are," lied Mr. Feldman. "But the law is the law. It's a Waterloo statute. Take a look." He reached into his breast pocket and produced a photocopy.

10

We gathered around Boom Boom and stared at the sheet.

Bylaw 14A, paragraph iv: No female personage shall be permitted to hold, or otherwise wield, a length of wood exceeding three feet, with the exceptions of mops, brooms, and butter churns.

Approved April 14, 1887. Yea 4, Nay 1.

"What does this dingus have to do with Alexia?" Boom Boom demanded.

"It doesn't even say anything about hockey," added Trent.

"A hockey stick is a length of wood," Mr. Feldman explained, trying to sound reasonable. "This law states that she can't carry a stick inside city limits." He chuckled. "You certainly wouldn't ask her to play without a stick."

"This is *so* bogus!" howled Jared.

"That stupid law is over a hundred years old!" added Josh.

Mr. Feldman got that superior-adult, snooty look on his face. "The law against murder is even older, and it still counts."

And that's how those rotten Waterloo types kicked Alexia out of the league. Oh, sure, we fought and hollered and complained. When Boom Boom's excitement level goes up, his English level goes down. He was thingamajigging and doohickeying at top volume.

I couldn't help noticing that Happer was standing behind his uncle, grinning at us with all thirty-two teeth. Now I understood what he'd meant by "Let's see how confident you are ten minutes from now." He'd known about this all along, that jerk!

Mr. Feldman kept saying, "The law is the law." But this wasn't about law. This was another big rip-off against us Marsers! How could the Stars play without Alexia? She was our captain, our second-best player! Her toughness and checking kept the other teams from trying to push us around.

I had one last card, and I played it. "You can't take Alexia away from us!" I argued. "That gives us only nine skaters and a goalie! The league minimum is ten skaters — or do we have to forfeit our playoff spot too?"

"Of course not," said Mr. Feldman. "That would be unfair."

Like he knew anything about fairness!

"The Stars will receive a replacement player," the president went on. "The next boy on the waiting list." He consulted his notebook. "Virgil Knox."

"Fragile!" chorused Jared and Cal in true pain.

We all knew Virgil from Waterloo Elementary School. People called him Fragile because he got a nosebleed every time the wind blew. He was the smallest, shortest, skinniest little dweeb in all of grade six. Eight-year-olds bullied him. In gym class, when choosing up teams, you would try to draft the gerbils out of the science lab before Virgil Knox.

Boom Boom was in such a white-hot rage that he was talking pure doohickeys. Even after Mr. Feldman had gone, the coach was still yelling at the empty space he used to be standing in. I'd never seen the team so mad. Faces flamed red, arms waved, fists clenched. We were all nuts — all except Alexia.

We knew she was upset because she was really quiet. But her expression was as bland as cottage cheese.

"What's everybody surprised about?" she said in a voice so low that we all stopped yelling and strained to hear her. "They always try to mess us up. This is just one more thing."

Josh, her twin, was almost in tears. "Aw, Lex, I'm so sorry! I can't believe they did this to you!"

"How are we going to play without you?" wailed Cal.

"How are we going to play *with* Fragile?" added Jared.

The drive home did nothing to lighten anybody's mood. When we rattled over the bridge into Mars, we were still yelling, and Alexia was still quiet.

||||| _Chapter 3_

Mars didn't have a fancy community center like the one in Waterloo. Our rink was outdoors, except for a small warm-up shack with a potbellied stove. The ice was lumpy in the cold weather and kind of mushy when it got warmer, like today. Most of the Stars' practices took place here. We got community center time too. But Mr. Feldman made sure we were always scheduled for six A.M., midnight, or Christmas morning.

They'd been working out for about ten minutes when I got there on Sunday. I almost croaked when I saw Alexia. Instead of practicing with the team, she was out of uniform, helping Coach Bolitsky run the various drills. I got depressed just looking at her. And the sight must have done the same for the other players, because the level of hustle out there was pretty pathetic. I wracked my brain for a headline idea, but all I could come up with was: *Zombies on Ice.*

I guess Boom Boom thought so too. He stopped the practice and called everyone to gather around.

"Listen up, you whosises!" the coach bawled. "I don't know what you call that thingamajig you've been doing, but I sure wouldn't call it hockey! Let's talk this out."

I turned on my tape recorder, but I knew I wasn't going to get anything I could use. The guys all started complaining at once.

The coach waved his arms for quiet. "I agree with you. We got heejazzed, and it isn't fair. But instead of feeling sorry for ourselves, think how hard this must be for Lex! She's taking this doojig like a man. I mean, a woman. I mean, a gizmo."

All eyes turned to Alexia. She looked fine. But I had a theory about that. This could be part of reverse volume control. I mean, she always looks kind of angry, even when everything is okay. Maybe when she goes beyond her boiling point, she starts looking more and more pleasant. I couldn't be sure — but if she ever started smiling, I was going to take cover in the warm-up shack.

Boom Boom went on. "So we're not going to talk

about this thingeroo anymore. Now, does anybody have anything to say that will help the team?"

There was a long silence, and then Jared raised his hand timidly. "I think we should get a Zamboni."

The coach's eyes bulged out even farther than normal. "A Zamboni? Why?"

Jared shrugged. "Everybody always complains that the ice isn't very good here. With a Zamboni, it would be better."

Jared comes up with a lot of dumb ideas. This late in the season, Boom Boom was good at handling him. "Well, Jared," he explained patiently, "thanks for your suggestion. But I don't think Mars has enough doohickeys in the budget."

"We could save money," Jared reasoned. "We wouldn't have to hire a Zamboni driver, because" — he looked sheepish — "because maybe I could do it."

Alexia brayed a laugh right in his face. "The truth comes out. You don't care about improving the ice. You just want a Zamboni so you can drive it."

Jared flushed. "When I was a little kid, it was my dream to be either a NASCAR racer or a hockey player. What do you get when you put them together? A Zamboni driver."

You could have heard a pin drop. It was during

that slack-jawed silence that we noticed a car pulling up to the curb.

The passenger door opened, and out stepped a pile of hockey equipment. We all stared. The only reason we knew there was a kid in there somewhere was because it started to walk toward us.

Out of the helmet came a piping voice: "Is this Mars?"

"No, it's Jupiter!" snarled Brian Azevedo, one of our defensemen.

The new arrival let himself onto the ice and glided up. It wasn't until he was right there with the other players that I recognized, deep inside the helmet, the mousy face of Virgil Knox.

Boom Boom regarded him. "You must be Whatsisname, our new thingamajig."

The kid looked so nervous that I don't even think he noticed the coach's unique way with words.

"Hello," he greeted. "Mr. Feldman told me to come here." He studied his skates. "You guys hate me, right?"

We were all so startled that nobody answered.

"What are you talking about?" roared Boom Boom. "Why should we hate you?"

"I'm replacing your captain," Virgil said tragically. "If I were you, I'd hate me."

It was a really uncomfortable moment. Oh, sure, none of us had anything personal against Virgil. We'd known the kid since kindergarten. He was an okay guy, for a little dweeb. But we hated what the league was doing to us. And Virgil was a symbol of that. So yeah, we kind of hated him.

Alexia broke the long silence. "Hey, hey, hey," she said sternly. "None of this is your fault. We want to welcome you to the Stars." She put an arm around Virgil's shoulders and beamed at the rest of us. "Don't we, guys?"

Uh-oh. This was getting scary. No way was that big grin the real thing.

Coach Bolitsky restarted the skating drill, and Josh sidled up to me at the boards. "What do you think of that?" he whispered in awe. "Man, I've never seen her so ticked off!"

Trent glided over. "I really admire your sister," he whispered to Josh. "I can't believe how well she's handling this. I thought she'd be chewing nails!"

Josh and I exchanged a knowing glance. Trent was a great hockey player, but he sure didn't know much about Alexia Colwin.

It all came out during bodychecking practice. As usual, Alexia ran this drill — even with no pads, she was the best hitter on the team. She was still smiling just as wide — maybe even wider. Then she took two powerful strides and knocked Trent flat on his back.

"Great thingie!" approved Boom Boom. "Next."

It was Mike Mozak, who centered our second unit. She hit him so hard that his helmet came off and bounced all the way to the opposite net.

She leveled Jared with a hip check and rammed her shoulder into Cal's chest with such force that he was lifted up and over her — and he was twice her size!

Coach Bolitsky liked all-out practices, but even he wasn't clapping so loudly anymore. "Take it easy, Lex," he called. "We can't win a game if half our players are in the whatchamacallit."

He meant *hospital*. But I was starting to think that a better translation might be *cemetery*.

A hush fell. The next Star in line was Virgil Knox. We all held our breath. This was going to be a massacre.

Boom Boom started forward. I think he was getting himself into position to stop her.

Virgil picked up the puck and started out. He was so short that the top of his stick was right up in his face. The puck scooted away from him, and he followed it, veering off course. His too-long stick rammed into the boards. The impact rattled all the way up the shaft and plowed the butt-end right into his face mask.

Bonk! The visor was pushed back against his nose.

Horror movies don't have that much blood. Now, we were all familiar with Virgil's famous nose-bleeds. But Boom Boom saw red all over the place and went nuts. He skated over and swooped the kid up like a bride.

"*Quick!*" he bellowed. "*Dial 9-1-whatchamacallit!*"

"I'm fine," gurgled Virgil. "I just need a Kleenex."

Coach Bolitsky was so surprised that the guy wasn't unconscious that he dropped him.

Trent skated over, flipped up Virgil's mask, and shoved a towel under his nose.

"It's okay, Coach," I assured Boom Boom. "This happens all the time."

"I'm a bleeder," added Virgil. "See? It's stopped already."

Relieved, the coach examined the ice. It was splattered crimson. "That's because you don't have any blood left!" To the rest of us, he said, "Go get shovels. Let's see if we can scrape up some of this whatsit."

Jared was all over that. "You know," he said, "this would clean up in about half a second if we had a Zamboni."

Virgil got back to his feet. He gazed mournfully at

the mess he'd made. "I'm sorry for bleeding on your rink," he mumbled into the towel. "Now I bet you hate me even more than before."

"We don't hate you," insisted Trent. But even he didn't sound a hundred percent convinced.

Chapter 4

After practice, the Stars all went to Mars Health Food for a team lunch. Everyone came except Virgil, whose mom was waiting to take him back home to Waterloo.

"Bring her along," invited the coach.

Virgil shook his head. "Everybody hates me. I'd only ruin everything."

"Nobody hates you!" Boom Boom roared right in the kid's face.

But Mrs. Knox was already honking the horn, so off he went.

To be honest, Virgil was the lucky one. The food at the Bolitskys' store and restaurant was really and truly awful. Today's meal consisted of tofu burritos, broccoli soup, and chilled cucumber juice.

You're probably wondering why we ate this terrible stuff. You sort of had to be a Star to understand. The coach and his wife were such great people. If it wasn't for them, Mars would never have gotten a hockey team. They treated us like gold. So it was a secret Stars' rule that we ate their health food and pretended to like it.

There we were, pushing the stuff around on our plates to make it look smaller, when Mrs. Bolitsky walked in from the kitchen.

The first sight of her was always kind of a jolt. As funny-looking as Boom Boom was, his wife was too gorgeous to describe. Most of the guys on the team couldn't even talk when she was around. Even now, when she was pregnant and — no offense — kind of lumpy, she still had that long black hair, those amazing eyes, a fantastic smile — you get the picture. She was awesome.

We all hustled to get her a chair and make her comfortable. Then we saw it. Our Mrs. B., the health food nut, was eating a triple-decker bacon and chili cheeseburger with the works! What's more, she couldn't wolf it down fast enough.

Cal held his nose and swallowed a mouthful of tofu. "Mrs. Bolitsky!" he exclaimed, shocked. "What are you eating? That's not a tofu burrito!"

"You said hamburgers are like poison!" added Kyle Ickes, Brian's defense partner.

"I don't know what's come over me!" She looked embarrassed, but not embarrassed enough to stop chomping. "Ever since I've been expecting, I don't like our health food anymore. You're not going to believe this, but to me it actually tastes *bad*!"

"No!" we chorused in horror. I'll bet any one of us would have traded our mothers for a bite of that burger!

"Yes!" she exclaimed earnestly. "And this is the only kind of food I eat now!"

Not entirely true. She also demolished a mountain of french fries with gravy, and washed it all down with a root beer ice-cream float. Here we sat, trying to slip tofu down to the dog, while she was having a junk food pig-out festival. Bits of chili and ketchup ran down her exquisite chin.

When she was finally done, she rushed to the kitchen and came back with an enormous paper sack. She began to rummage around inside it. There was a clinking sound like marbles in a bag — but even more hauntingly familiar. At last, her hand emerged, daintily holding between her thumb and forefinger — a jawbreaker.

A jawbreaker!

You may not know this about me, but I happen to be the number-one customer of the jawbreaker industry. That's how I got the name Chipmunk —

from having my face all puffed out because there was always a great big ball of candy tucked in my cheek.

Then came Black Monday. Dentist appointment. Eleven cavities. I hadn't had a jawbreaker since the All-Star break. And to see one! Not just any old one, but a Grape-ola Mega-Bomb with real fruit juice explosions inside! It was like taking a guy dying of thirst in the desert and teasing him with a glass of water.

I watched her perfect cheek bulge out with that Mega-Bomb. It was almost like she was the one named Chipmunk, not me.

I know what you're thinking. The Bolitskys were great people. I could just ask her for one. But life isn't that simple. My next dental checkup was coming in three weeks. If I got cavities *now*, my whole six months of torture, of flossing until my gums shredded, of brushing so hard I dislocated my shoulder, would be for nothing. And then I'd never see another jawbreaker for sure.

Trent choked down the last of his cucumber juice and sighed. "I've got to tell you, guys, I'm worried about the game on Saturday. It's going to hurt losing Lex. And who knows what we're going to do with Fragile. But mostly I'm worried about *us*. We're so down in the dumps that I don't think we're ready to put out the kind of effort it takes to win in the play-offs."

"Well, can you really blame us?" complained Josh. He was a pretty mild-mannered kid, but he was taking this harder than any of us. Alexia was his twin sister, after all. "I say we just don't go on Saturday. Show them what they can do with their stupid play-offs."

"That's exactly what they're hoping we'll do, *bonehead*," said Alexia in reverse volume control. "They *want* us out."

"We're going to get eliminated on Saturday anyway," Brian said miserably. "Josh just wants to go out *our* way — thumbing our noses at Feldman and the league."

"Forget it," countered Trent. "That would give them the ammunition they need to throw the Stars out permanently."

It was Boom Boom's coaching style to let the team argue for a while before putting his two cents in. I turned up the volume on my tape recorder so I wouldn't miss a single word.

He said, "I played in the NHL for sixteen hee-jazzes, and never — not once — did I make the play-offs. Every time I was on a winning doojig, I got traded into last place. I only know one thingamabob: If you get a chance to be in the playoffs, you say whatsit."

"You say yes," translated his wife around her jaw-breaker.

You could just see the Stars' faces change. Boom Boom didn't talk much, and even less of it was in English. But what he did say cut straight to the heart of the matter.

"You're right, Coach," said Josh, shamefaced. "What are we going to do to beat the Bruins?"

"Maybe we can get Fragile to bleed on them," joked Cal.

Trent groaned. "What are we going to do about that guy? He's going to get killed out there!"

"I'll tell you one thing," promised Brian darkly. "If he says one more time that everybody hates him, I'm going to start hating him!"

"Lay off Virgil," Alexia said protectively. "He's a cute little guy, and I like him."

"Oh, sure," challenged her brother sarcastically. "And you weren't about to take his head off in the bodychecking drill."

"She didn't have to," put in Trent. "He did it himself."

"Oh, yeah," said Boom Boom. "He really ate wood. I thought he was whatchamacallit."

"Dead," translated his wife.

That got Cal chuckling. And watching him giggling made the rest of us laugh too. For the first time since the league meeting, the mood lifted itself a teeny bit above rock bottom.

I thought of a one-word headline: *Hope*.

And that gave me an idea.

Chapter 5 \\\\\\\\\\

The school bus picked us up every weekday at eight o'clock. The Waterloo jerks called it *Pathfinder*, after the NASA space mission to Mars. But for once I wouldn't be there to listen to the usual unfunny jokes. Seven o'clock Monday morning found me on Waterloo Transit. My destination: the public library. When the janitor came to open the building, there I was, sitting on the front steps, waiting to get in.

I didn't trust Mr. Feldman as far as I could throw him. I wanted to see this so-called law for myself.

Now, doing research isn't my favorite part of being a reporter — too boring and all that. But it's important. When I'm on staff at *Sports Illustrated*, I might need to find out stuff. Like Wayne Gretzky's scoring records, the height and weight of the Stanley Cup, or what year hockey changed from six skaters to five (there used to be an extra guy, called the rover, positioned between the two defensemen. But that was super-long ago).

So up I went, four flights of stairs, to the musty old attic where they kept the town archives. It took forever, but I finally found that stupid old statute about women carrying sticks.

There I sat, choking on dust and rage. You know what that dumb law was all about? A hundred and thirteen years ago, some lady got her mule stuck in the mud. She used a big stick to try to lever him out. But the mule was so heavy that she dropped dead from the strain. So this statute was supposed to protect women from hurting themselves doing heavy work. And they'd never changed the law, so it was still in force. That's why, more than a century later, Alexia was out and Fragile was in!

I was twice as mad as before. Talk about unfair! Luckily, the Stars had a team reporter. I could use the sports section of the *Gazette* to expose this big rip-off to the world.

But the next *Gazette* didn't come out until after the quarterfinals this weekend! The Stars would have to play *without* Alexia and *with* Virgil! By the next paper, they could be exactly where the Waterloo types wanted them — eliminated! Sometimes a once-a-month paper was worse than no paper at all!

There was only one thing for me to do. I had to go see the mayor. The government made that law, and the government could unmake it.

I know what you're thinking: How can a kid get an appointment with the mayor? Well, I used to have a paper route. I knew where he lived.

I didn't know the part about how late he sleeps on Mondays. I think I woke him up. He came to the door in his bathrobe, and he wasn't really pleased to see me.

"I hope I'm not disturbing you, Mayor Sloan." I wanted to get on his good side, so I added, "Nice pajamas."

He stifled a major yawn. "I've always got time for one of our young citizens."

"Well, actually, I'm not a citizen of Waterloo," I admitted. "I'm Chipmunk Adelman, from Mars."

He groaned. "Oh, right. Mars. What can I do for you, son?"

I told him about the 1887 law, and how it was keeping Alexia out of the playoffs.

To my surprise, he was really cool about it. He invited me in and gave me a glass of orange juice while he made a note of my complaint on his computer.

"I'm glad you brought this to my attention, Chipmunk," he told me. "Like most towns, Waterloo has a lot of out-of-date laws. But we can't strike them down if people like you don't tell us about them."

I was thrilled. "You mean this is going to get struck down?"

"Absolutely," he assured me. "I'll start the process in motion as soon as I get to the office."

"Wow!" I exclaimed. "That's fast! So it's not going to take very long at all, is it?"

The mayor smiled. "Once the hearing takes place, it's an instant thing." His fingers danced over the keyboard. "The first available hearing date is — let's see — December fourteenth. Nine A.M. sharp."

The letdown was so huge that I'm amazed I didn't pass out right on his floor. "But that's too late for the playoffs! That's halfway through next season!"

He chuckled. "This is government, you know. There are procedures we have to follow."

Outside it had started to sleet. The mayor patted my slumping shoulder. "Let me get dressed. I'll give you a ride to school."

"Do I have to wait for a hearing date?" I asked bitterly. "Because then you should drop me off at college graduation."

He laughed and laughed. I didn't see what was so funny.

We got to school just as the Waterloo bus was letting out.

"Where were you, Chipmunk?" asked Josh. He frowned as my ride pulled back out into the road. "Wasn't that Mayor Sloan?"

I sighed. "Remind me never to work in government," I told him. "They can't do anything until it's too late for it to matter."

‖‖‖‖‖ *Chapter 6*

The community center had playoff fever. There wasn't an empty seat or a space to stand in as the opening face-off approached.

A lot of Marsers always came out to watch the Stars. But today they were outnumbered by five times as many Waterloo fans. Dozens of flashbulbs made the stands glitter. A carnival atmosphere was in full force. Quarterfinal Saturday was always a big afternoon.

There was a lot for a sportswriter to report on. But the sight that caught my eye was Alexia. There she stood, alone at the Stars' bench, ramrod straight like a palace guard. But where a guard would hold a rifle, she brandished a long-handled mop.

As wired up as I was, I had to cheer. It was the perfect in-your-face to Mr. Feldman. That idiotic law said she couldn't carry a stick. But a mop was on the list of things that were okay.

The referee skated up, confused. "What are you doing with a mop?"

She shrugged. "I couldn't find a butter churn."

The Stars mobbed their captain, congratulating her like she'd just scored a hat trick. The ref skated away, shaking his head.

Boom Boom slapped Alexia on the back. "We're sure going to miss you out there, kid."

Were we ever! In the first sixty seconds of the warm-up, Virgil Knox ate wood again, and we had another bloodbath. It was such a mess that they had to clear the ice and bring the Zamboni back out.

Jared leaned over the boards, lost in admiration. "Look at that guy," he said wistfully, pointing at the driver. "He's got it all. I can only imagine what must be going through his mind at a moment like this."

"He's probably wondering how this much blood could come out of one little nose," said Brian.

"You hate me for this, don't you?" bubbled Fragile. "You hate me even more than before."

"We don't hate you; we love you," Alexia assured him. "But the ice maintenance people — *they* hate you."

While the cleanup continued, Coach Bolitsky hacksawed the top ten inches off Virgil's too-long stick.

Finally, after a twenty-minute delay, the game could begin.

With a shorter stick, Virgil didn't butt-end himself in the face anymore. But as a hockey player, he was about as useful as sunscreen to an earthworm. He was so small that his blood-spattered Stars jersey hung down to his ankles like an evening gown. His sleeves were rolled up so many times that he appeared to be wearing water wings. He was an okay skater, but his legs were short, and he was pretty slow. Definitely not the guy you'd want to replace Alexia Colwin. Especially not against the Bruins.

The Baker's Auto Body team was big and tough. They'd finished third overall in the standings this year, mostly because of that big-muscle style of play. Their captain was a caveman named Willis Gerard, and he only had one weakness: He was afraid of Alexia. It killed me to see what a happy surprise it was for him that Alexia wasn't suited up.

"One at a time," he promised Trent, "I'm going to mash your whole team into the ice."

"You wouldn't have the guts to say that if my sister were playing!" bellowed Josh.

"Do your worst," invited Alexia from the bench.

Sure enough, on the opening face-off, Willis flattened Trent with a dirty elbow that the referee missed.

"That's one!" sneered the Bruins' captain once the play was finally whistled down.

Alexia shrugged. "You got lucky." But on the next play, it was Jared's turn. Willis cut him off on a race for the puck and slammed him hard into the boards.

"That's two!" He grinned.

Alexia dismissed this with a wave of her mop. "The Stars aren't afraid of a big doofus like you."

"*I'm* afraid of a big doofus like him!" whispered Virgil urgently.

I could see Fragile's point. Here was Alexia making the guy mad while everybody else had to face the consequences.

But the next victim turned out to be Brian. Willis blindsided him into the goalpost and stole the puck.

Now, Willis Gerard was more than just a goon. He was a great offensive hockey player. He fed his left winger, who got off a pretty good wrist shot. Josh made a tough blocker save.

"Clear the dingus!" roared Coach Bolitsky.

"The rebound!" I translated.

That was easier said than done. Kyle got his stick on the puck and — *wham!* — Willis crunched him into the corner. Bruins swarmed like locusts, muscling the Stars out of the play. Willis positioned himself in front of the net.

"Move him out of here!" Josh cried urgently. "I can't see the puck!"

But not even Trent and Jared together could push the Bruins' bull of a captain. Pretty soon, a defenseman let loose a booming slapshot from the point. With Willis screening him, Josh had no chance. 1–0, Bruins.

"We beat you before; we'll beat you again," Willis sneered right in Trent's face.

But you don't get to be a three-time MVP by letting yourself get psyched out by a bully. The next time Trent got the puck, he put a move on Willis that left the guy flat-footed.

"Spin-o-rama!" I cheered out my headline idea, while Trent blasted past Willis.

It would have been a clean breakaway. Willis had no choice but to reach out his stick and yank Trent's skates out from under him. The Mars fans howled for a penalty.

Up went the referee's hand. "Two minutes for tripping!" he barked. Mars Health Food would have a man advantage.

How should I describe the Stars' power play? It was definitely nonaverage. The backbone of it all was Kyle Ickes, who brought the puck out of the zone. He caught sight of Josh, who was signaling him to attack from the left wing, where the defense was weakest.

You're probably wondering how a guy can lead a rush and still keep an eye on his own goalie, who's *behind* him. The thing is, Kyle was the greatest backward skater in Slapshot League history. And since he couldn't skate forward to save his life, all his rushes were backward.

Down the ice he reversed. To see where he was going, he looked at the car mirror that was superglued to his face mask. Sure, there were a lot of weird things about the Stars. But you go with what works.

Just before the blue line, Kyle passed off to Brian — did I mention *he* only skated forward? But Brian was the fastest Star. He flashed into the Bruins' zone, drawing their defensemen out of position.

Suddenly, Trent swung out behind him. "I'm open!"

Drop pass! Slapshot!

The Bruins' goalie dove for it, but he was too late. Tie game, 1–1.

The headline formed in my mind, and I barked it out during the celebration. *"First-Ever Stars' Playoff Goal!"*

The joy didn't last long. That power-play goal sprung Willis from the penalty box. Pretty soon, the Bruins' captain lined up Mike Mozak with a hip check that sent poor Mike sprawling into the goal-post.

"That's five!" chortled Willis.

"Big deal," Alexia retorted. "You haven't gotten Cal yet."

She probably thought that one was safe. Cal was the biggest Star and, after her, the best bodychecker. But that didn't stop Willis. On the next face-off, he made a rhino charge at Cal, catching him behind the goal. The burly Marser bounced off the boards and flipped backward clear over the net, knocking Josh flat. With our goalie immobilized, it was nothing for a Bruins' winger to pop the puck into the top corner.

Suddenly, the Bruins were back in the lead.

Chapter 7 ⎰⎰⎰⎰⎰

The score was still 2–1 at the first intermission.

"Will you quit needling that guy Willis!" Cal roared at Alexia in the locker room. "Every time you open your mouth, one of us gets clobbered!"

Alexia looked disgusted. "Somebody has to help you wimps stick up for yourselves, since I can't be on the ice to do it for you."

"Nobody panic," said Coach Bolitsky with his usual good sense. "We're only down one dingus. My wife will be here any minute with her whatcha-macallit."

Since it was going to be tough playing without Alexia, Mrs. Bolitsky had been recruited to come to the game and sit in the back row of bleachers for the full-ice view. Now we waited for her scouting report.

She made kind of a grand entrance. First her hot dog arrived. It was eighteen inches long, supported by two buns, and dripping mustard and ketchup. She had it carefully balanced in her arms so one hand was left free for her king-size milk shake. Remember — this was a woman who used to nibble on bean sprouts and think she was eating. Now she had to turn sideways to get her dinner *and* her stomach through the door. It was an amazing sight.

"All right," barked her husband, all business. "What's your report?"

"The mustard isn't tangy enough," she said thoughtfully, "but the homemade piccalilli is aces."

We all stared at her, but no one had the guts to ask a question, not even Boom Boom.

The buzzer sounded to call the teams back to the ice.

The second period was the chance for the Stars to kick into overdrive, pull even with the Bruins, and then blow them away. At least that's what I recorded in my notes. And we might even have done that if we'd had Alexia.

In real life, we had Virgil, and lots of him. From a defensive standpoint, he was useless. When his opposing winger got the puck, Fragile was as far away as it was possible to be without leaving the arena. But on offense, he was worse than useless. Every time Trent started a rush, the little guy always managed to be in the way. Jared actually tripped over him. He was a menace.

At the bench, Boom Boom had some coaching tips for Virgil.

"When we've got the doojig, stay in your whatsit, and make sure you know where all your doohickeys are."

The panic was plain on our newest winger's face.

Alexia spent the second period bugging Willis Gerard.

"What's the matter, Willis?" she sang out sweetly. "I thought you were going to mash our whole team. Or are you too chicken?"

That made Willis furious. A minute later, he lined up Jared and plowed him over, leaving him in a heap at center ice. "That's ten!" he celebrated.

"No, it isn't." Alexia laughed. "You got him already. You're still stuck back at nine, loser."

Jared picked himself up and skated over to Josh. "Will you tell your sister to cut it out?" he demanded. "She'll get us all killed!"

Josh shrugged. "Lay off Lex. Think about how terrible it must feel to have to sit this game out."

"That's easy for you to say," Jared complained. "You're safe. Willis could never come after the goalie."

Wrong. On the very next play, the Bruins' captain charged in on goal. Right in front of the referee, he made a big show of pretending to trip. On the seat of his pants, he slid through the crease, hitting Josh below the knees. Our goalie went down like a sack of potatoes. Only his mask kept him from flattening his face on the ice.

Boom Boom was up on the bench, and his ponytail was soaring. "That's a thingamajig!"

"A penalty!" I translated.

The ref waved it off. "Accident."

"Yeah, an accident." Willis grinned. "I'm a really clumsy guy." Then, as he skated by our bench, he sneered at Alexia, *"That's* ten."

Man, were the Stars ever mad! There's an unwritten rule in hockey that you never let anyone mess with your goalie. I could see Trent and Jared hanging around the Bruins' captain, waiting for a chance to put a little something extra on a body check. This was a big mistake. With them out of position, and Virgil in the wrong place as usual, Bruins stormed over the blue line on a four-man rush.

Pow! It was a booming slapshot from the slot. Josh never had a chance. And suddenly, the Stars were down by two.

The mood was somber in the locker room at the second intermission. It sure looked like the Stars'

Cinderella story was about to wind up in a very short playoff. There was still a whole period to go, but everyone was acting like this game was over. Normally the team would have been hounding Coach Bolitsky, begging for tips on how to get back in this thing. Instead, they sat silently, faces long.

Even Trent's mind was elsewhere. "You know, Lex," he told the Stars' captain, "you weren't exactly a big help today."

I could almost hear the gears clicking as Alexia shifted into reverse volume control.

"Gee, Ruben, you're a genius. What was your first clue? The fact that I don't have skates on?"

"You know what I mean," he growled. "Why did you have to challenge Willis to clobber his way through the team?"

She looked at him pityingly. "What's the object of a hockey game? To score goals, right? Well, if a guy is running around trying to knock people down, what's he *not* doing?"

Trent looked at her with round-eyed respect. "Are you telling me you did that on purpose to keep him going for the body instead of the puck?"

She nodded. "That's right, hotshot. And if I hadn't, you'd be down five goals, instead of just two."

Mrs. Bolitsky walked into the locker room. Her giant hot dog and milk shake were gone. She was

46

working on dessert now. I stared. There was a bump in her right cheek as big as an acorn. But when she turned her head, I realized there was an identical bump on the other side.

I was blown away. Our Mrs. B. was attempting a double-jawbreaker gambit! Even at the height of my jawbreaker career, I never dared to go that far. It was the candy equivalent of tightrope walking over Niagara Falls!

"Listen up, you whosises!" barked the coach. To his wife he said, "Let's hear the scouting report."

And this time she really did have a scouting report. She unfolded a piece of paper from her pocket and began to read from her notes.

"Grrbl vrr blrr mummfl vrr krrflntz vrrfl . . ."

And the moral of the story is: Two jawbreakers at the same time may be great for your taste buds, but they're not too good for public speaking.

The buzzer sounded. This was it. The third period. What a *Sports Illustrated* moment! It was do-or-die for the Stars!

Chapter 8 ⎪⎪⎪⎪⎪

Willis Gerard spent the third period skating around staring into face guards. I think he was trying to figure out which player he hadn't decked yet. Every time he approached a Star, Alexia would call out, "Not him — you got him already."

And then something amazing happened. Brian shot the puck behind the Bruins' net, and their goalie scrambled back to get it. But just as he made his clearing pass, Willis swerved out in front. I guess he was trying to figure out if Mike Mozak was on the "already hit" list. Whatever the reason, the puck bounced off Willis's leg and trickled into the empty net.

It was such a flukey play that we hardly even celebrated. But talk about *huge*! The Stars, who had seemed dead in the water a minute ago, were now only a single goal behind.

On the bench, Alexia whacked Trent across the back of his helmet with her mop.

"You see that, hotshot?" she said in reverse volume control. "That was a gift from heaven. Now, if you don't go out there and tie it up *this minute*, you'd better look over your shoulder for the rest of your life, because I'll be coming after you."

Trent stared at her. "Are you threatening me?"

"In front of witnesses," she confirmed.

I know it sounds crazy, but I've got the whole conversation on tape. And the weirdest part is it unfolded exactly the way she ordered it.

Trent won the face-off with a lightning flick of his wrists. He tapped the puck between Willis's legs and stepped around him like a square-dancing *do-si-do*. Then a burst of speed, and he was gone.

I leaped up in my seat. All the Stars fans did. When Trent Ruben works up a head of steam, nobody in the league can touch him. And nobody did. The deke he put on the first defenseman was a stick-handling masterpiece. The second defenseman actually moved to get out of Trent's way.

Trent fired a snap shot that was so perfectly aimed I don't think Dominik Hasek could have stopped it.

He picked the top corner of the net with the precision of a diamond cutter.

"Tie game!" I shrieked, sending the sound level of my tape recorder into the danger zone. The Mars fans were going nuts.

I couldn't believe it. This had to be the first time in hockey history that anyone was *bullied* into scoring the tying goal. What a great human interest story for *Sports Illustrated*, or even the *Gazette*. Too bad I didn't dare write it. Alexia would kill me for sure.

I thought Willis Gerard was going to blow a gasket. You could barely see his red face behind his steamed-up visor. But instead of focusing on regaining the lead, he put all his effort into finding that eleventh Star — the one he hadn't knocked down yet.

Alexia got on his case and wouldn't let go. "Ten isn't eleven," she reminded him cheerfully. "What's the matter, Willis? Can't you finish what you've started?"

The Bruins' captain roared his frustration to the bleachers. *"Who's left?"*

Alexia wagged her finger at him like a mother scolding a baby. "Uh, uh, uh — that would be telling."

But then Willis's dilemma solved itself. For right in front of his cloudy visor struggled a shrimpy little kid in an oversize, blood-spattered Stars uniform. The eleventh man, Virgil Knox.

Even from my spot behind the players' bench, I could see Willis's eyes lock onto Virgil like a heat-seeking missile.

Alexia saw it too. "*Virgil!*" she warned.

But it was no use. Willis was one of the best players in the league, and Fragile was too small, too slow, and too clueless.

Three powerful strides and the Bruins' captain was breathing down Fragile's skinny neck. The big bully lowered his shoulder and braced himself to step into that poor little kid.

And he missed. I can't explain how it happened, but I can tell you what it *looked* like. Willis left his feet, passed right through Fragile without ever touching him, and *wham*! I swear the whole building shook when he hit those boards. They had to stop the clock to scrape him off the wall.

He was okay, but the wind was knocked so far out of him that he probably wasn't going to start breathing again till Thursday. By Slapshot League rules, he had to come out of the game.

The Bruins' coach was horrified. "That's not fair! How can a team play without its captain?"

Alexia spread her arms wide. "Beats me."

By this time, Virgil had finally managed to chug

his way back to the Stars' bench. I stuck my tape recorder in front of his face. Maybe he could explain what happened.

"Oh, no," he lamented. "Now the other team hates me too."

Boom Boom was really excited. "This is it!" he raved. "We lost our captain, and they lost theirs! Now it's an even thingeroo!" His praying-mantis eyes traveled to the clock. "We have a minute and thirty-seven whatchamacallits to score!"

You could just see the players coming back to life. These were the Stars that we knew and loved. Brian anchored the rush with speed and confidence. Kyle's backward attacks confused the defenders. The forwards made precision passes, opening up great scoring chances. Josh was solid as a rock in the net.

The clock showed thirty seconds to play. Oh, man, I wanted a goal! Sure, we would still have a chance in overtime. But right now the Stars were totally dominating the play. This was our best shot at finishing off the Bruins before they could regroup.

Then Baker's Auto Body caught the Stars off guard halfway through a line change.

"*Go back!*" bellowed Boom Boom.

But it was too late. Our first line was out of position and out of play.

Heroically, Trent stopped on a dime and hurled himself at the puck carrier in a desperation diving poke-check.

The puck came loose and dribbled over to Virgil, who stared at it like it was a live grenade. After all, this was the first time he'd touched it all game, and there were only fifteen seconds left in the third period.

"*Shoot it!*" It came from me, the coach, and about half the players.

And he did — a weird, clumsy golf shot that slid to the corner in slow motion.

Well, talk about a stampede! Everybody forgot their positions and went after that puck. Pretty soon, two whole teams were crammed into the corner, digging away.

Eight seconds! Seven — six —

Big Cal muscled himself free and snared the puck with his stick. He looked out in front for Mike, his center. But since all this was happening in the middle of a botched line change, Mike was still on the bench. The only one out there was Jared, who was supposed to be on the *other* line.

"I'm open!" Jared banged his stick on the ice.

Four — three — two —

Cal feathered a perfect pass. Jared didn't even

stop it — there was no time. He whacked it past the Bruins' goalie and into the net a split second before the clock ran out.

Final score: 4–3, Stars.

The Stars from Mars were moving on to the next round.

IIIII Chapter 9

"All right," said Mr. Ping, the science teacher. "Who stole Mars?"

He meant the planet, not the town. We were gathered around the table model of the solar system. Mercury, Venus, and all the other planets were there — except one. The fourth orbit contained a banana.

There was a lot of giggling and snickering going on. Those Waterloo types thought there was nothing more hilarious than making fun of Mars. And we Marsers had no choice but to suck it up and take it.

Happer elbowed Oliver, who raised his hand. "Mr. Ping, isn't that Mars over there?"

He pointed to the back of the lab. Sure enough, there was the red planet, dangling at the end of a hangman's noose. It was riddled with bullet holes; a long feathered arrow pierced it; toy sticks of dynamite were strapped to it; and the thing rested on a miniature electric chair. A hand-lettered sign on the rope above it proclaimed: MARTIAN PLAYOFF HOPES.

Happer and Oliver led the applause, and even Mr. Ping chuckled a little. The only Marser who laughed was Cal, and he stopped when Alexia took the banana and crammed it into his mouth.

Trent stuck up for us. "Last time I checked, the Stars were going on to play the Sharks in the semifinals. So our playoff hopes don't seem too bad, do they?"

"In your dreams!" sneered Happer. "No Martian will ever lay an alien finger on the Feldman Cup. That's my prediction, and I'm standing by it."

"Pretty soon you might be sitting on it." That was Alexia — quieter than quiet. But everybody heard it.

I could see Happer and Oliver were pretty confident though. They had every right to be. Right after our game, the defending champions had crushed the Flames 7–1. Five of those goals had been scored by Happer Feldman.

"Your days as MVP are over, Ruben," Happer informed Trent. "I went to Wayne Gretzky's hockey clinic over spring break."

"You mean hockey clinic teaches you how to be a bigmouthed doofus?" Alexia asked mildly.

Oliver glared at her. "Big talk from someone who's out of the league."

"I had three private lessons with Wayne Gretzky himself," Happer went on. "We spent the whole time working on my wrist shot."

I'll bet Trent was dying to tell him, "Who cares?" But five goals in a playoff game — that was pretty convincing proof to back up his bragging.

"Today we're beginning a unit on astronomy," Mr. Ping was saying. "Some of you might be tempted to make jokes just because the town next to ours happens to be called Mars. All right, you've had your fun. Now, let's try to take this seriously, shall we?"

Well, you can pretty much figure out what happened. No one took it seriously. Every time Mars got mentioned, somebody delivered a loud moose call. And it wasn't just Mars. Those jerks cracked up over *planet*, *orbit*, *asteroid*, *star*, *nebula*, *satellite*, and even *clouds*.

"Aw, come on!" I exploded. "You've got clouds here in Waterloo, too, you know!"

"Actually," piped up the munchkin voice of Virgil Knox, "there's no reason to associate clouds with Mars. Earth is a much cloudier world."

There was dead silence. I turned around in my chair and stared at the little guy. Was this his way of trying to stick up for Mars? Or was he just missing the point, as usual?

That was it for Mr. Ping. "Could we please concentrate on science? When you hear the same joke a hundred times, it just isn't funny anymore."

Tell that to the Waterloo jerks. The moose calls and snickers stopped. Now whenever Mr. Ping said "Mars," they bounced a spitball off my head or nailed me with a crumpled-up piece of paper.

I ignored them. I ignored Mr. Ping too. I had more important things to do. The new *Gazette* was coming out on Wednesday. I was going to write an article that would blow the roof off the Waterloo Slapshot League and their 1887 law. They wouldn't get away with keeping Alexia out of the playoffs. When people read this, they would be just as outraged as me. I had the perfect headline:

WHATEVER HAPPENED TO FAIRNESS?

by Clarence "Chipmunk" Adelman,
Gazette Sports Reporter

I knew my biggest challenge as a writer would be to make everybody see how dumb that old law was. So I really gave it to them there:

That law against women carrying sticks has nothing to do with hockey. The Slapshot League

wants Alexia out because they're afraid that the Stars are getting too good. They're just sore because Mars made the playoffs in their first year.

We can't let the league get away with this. Even Mayor Sloan agrees that it's a stupid law. The Stars' next playoff game is on Saturday. Phone Mr. Feldman. His number is unlisted, but it's 555-8406. Put Alexia Colwin back on the ice where she belongs. . . .

I polished off the rest of the article just before the bell. I was pretty proud of it. I'll bet a few hundred phone calls would help Mr. Feldman learn his lesson.

I took the stairs three at a time and caught Mrs. Spiro just a couple of steps away from the teachers' coffee room. She was the editor of the Waterloo Elementary School *Gazette* and also my English teacher.

"Here's my article! It's ready!" I panted. "We can print it a couple of days early so everybody can — you know — read it before the weekend."

She started to give my page the quick once-over. But pretty soon she was reading it word for word. And frowning.

"Clarence, I can't print this."

"But you have to!" I pleaded. "It's the only way to get justice!"

She sighed. "Clarence, you can't make wild accusations against someone and then publish his phone number and encourage people to harass him. It's against the law."

"You always said that a good reporter stands up for what's right," I argued.

She must have wanted her coffee really badly, because she looked extra annoyed. "If you write something proper, it will be included in this month's *Gazette.* If not, we will go to press without a sports section. Is that clear?"

That's the whole problem with teachers. When they're talking in front of a class, it's a perfect world. But when it comes to real life, you're not allowed to do *anything*.

I was so mad that I was walking up and down the hall talking to myself. How could I write a nice little article about who played who and who scored what? I'd be ignoring the biggest rip-off in the history of the Slapshot League. It would be like saying a house has pink frilly curtains and leaving out the fact that the whole place is on fire!

But there was no way I could ever sneak this article past Mrs. Spiro. She was so nuts about wasting paper that she read everything a zillion times before printing the *Gazette.*

What could I do?

||||| _Chapter 10_

The Stars' next practice was at the community center after school on Tuesday. That's another way Mr. Feldman socked it to us. Our slot was three-thirty to four-thirty. But since the bell didn't ring until three-thirty, we'd have to waste a huge chunk of our ice time just getting there and getting dressed.

We had a system. At three-twenty-five, every single Star asked to visit the washroom. They grabbed their duffels out of their lockers, suited up in the stalls (except for their skates), and waited out the rest of the day. The second the bell rang, it was a footrace for the exit. There in the front driveway was Coach Bolitsky in the Mars Health Food van. We piled into the back, and Boom Boom burned rubber for the community center. It sounds crazy, but it was the only way we could make the most of our hour.

Today was the first time Virgil got to participate in this frantic drill. I guess nobody told him that the team bus was piled high with sacks of health food. He dove in headfirst and plowed his face into a fifty-pound bag of granola.

Anyway, when we pulled up in front of the community center and Boom Boom opened up the back of the van, he saw his entire team covered in blood and cereal.

Boom Boom was horrified. "He ate wood again?"

"No," said Alexia. "Just granola."

"Now even the coach hates me," bubbled Virgil.

The team had barely stepped onto the ice when Alexia raised her hand. "Coach, why don't we start with the bodychecking drill?"

Boom Boom thought it over. "Fair enough. Okay, forwards on the left, whosises on the right —"

Alexia shook her head. "*Special* bodychecking drill. Kind of an experiment. Just Virgil and me."

Uh-oh . . .

Boom Boom must have been thinking the same thing. "Uh — I don't think that's such a good whatsit," he said carefully. "After all, Virgil doesn't have the — uh — experience, or the — uh — doohickeys —"

"It's not his fault what's happened —" Josh added.

"Tell you what," put in Trent. "*I* volunteer to be the punching bag for your experiment —"

Alexia was totally disgusted. "Are you guys finished?"

"But, Lex —" persisted Boom Boom.

It was Fragile himself who sealed the deal. "No, Coach," the little guy said bravely. "This is something I have to do. Otherwise, everyone will hate me forever."

Virgil picked up the puck and started skating toward Alexia in that weird, hunched-over style of his. Alexia closed in on him in two confident strides and lowered her shoulder for a crushing check.

"We're going to need the Zamboni," mumbled Jared.

"We might even need *two* Zambonis," amended Cal.

I admit it. I closed my eyes.

When I opened them again, Alexia was flat on her face sliding along the ice and Virgil was chugging past her.

"She missed!" whispered Brian in disbelief.

"Lex doesn't miss!" added Josh, wide-eyed.

Alexia scrambled back up. "Let's try this again," she said in reverse volume control.

So they started over. This time she lined him up

for a hip check that would have sent any of the other players flying. But somehow, Fragile managed to squeak through it.

"Well, I'll be a monkey's gizmo!" exclaimed Boom Boom in awe.

Finally, Alexia went straight at Virgil like she was trying to mow him down. She ended up skating right over him. He was bent so low that his helmet never even got touched.

Virgil turned to the coach, clueless as usual. "When does the body check happen?"

The team was stunned. I figured Alexia would be spitting lava by now. But when she glided up, she was grinning from ear to ear.

"I knew it!" she crowed. "*That's* why Willis blew that check last game. Virgil is unhittable!"

"Unhittable?" echoed Brian. "There's no such thing!"

"See for yourselves," she invited.

And they did. One by one, the whole team went after Virgil. They got the same results as Willis and Alexia. Even Boom Boom tried — a real NHL player! He nearly knocked himself unconscious against the door of the penalty box.

The team was stumped. Alexia thought it was Virgil's height that made everybody miss. Trent insisted it was his bent-over skating style. Josh suggested that Virgil was such a scaredy-cat that he had a natural instinct to duck whenever danger was near.

But whatever the reason, an unhittable player was surely a good thing to have in a hockey game — even if the unhittable player happened to stink at everything except not getting hit.

"Virgil," called the coach, still woozy from his accident. "Come over and join the rest of the whatsit."

Virgil struggled over, devastated. "I messed up, didn't I?"

"You didn't mess up," the coach explained patiently.

"In fact," Alexia added, "your job on this team just got a whole lot bigger."

We invited Virgil to come with the team to Mars Health Food for our after-practice meeting and snack. But once again he turned us down.

Trent guessed his reasoning. "Virgil, nobody hates you. Didn't you notice that Coach Bolitsky spent the whole practice working just with you?"

Virgil nodded sadly. "I kept the coach away from everybody else for a whole hour. I'm trouble."

You just can't win an argument with Fragile. Sometimes I think he *wants* to be hated. And anyway, there were zucchini sloppy joes on the menu, so the kid was probably better off going straight home.

The stuff was already on the table, steaming and gross, when we got to the restaurant. Beautiful Mrs. Bolitsky — who was getting rounder every day — greeted us at the door. She was on her way out to the garbage, struggling with a huge shopping bag.

It just goes to show how focused a reporter gets when he's onto a big story. I almost missed the clinking sound that could only come from one thing. I ran after her and grabbed the bag a quarter of an inch from the Dumpster.

"Mrs. B. — *no*! How could you throw out all those jawbreakers?"

She looked really sad. "I know, Chipmunk. But I have to get rid of them."

"But *why*?" I just about wailed.

"I had a dentist appointment today, and I have a cavity! I haven't had a cavity since I was a little girl! My dentist says it's because of the jawbreakers."

Jawbreakers cause cavities. Well, what do you know.

Then she offered the fox the keys to the chicken coop.

"Would you like to have them, Chipmunk?" she asked, holding out the bag.

I wish I could say it was her beautiful brown eyes that won me over. But the fact is I would have taken those jawbreakers from the ugliest baboon in the jungle. They were *jawbreakers*! They were as much a part of me as my ears!

Yeah, I know. I couldn't eat any of them. I had a dentist appointment coming up, too — in a little less than two weeks. And for me the heat was on. If Dr. Mendez detected even the slightest hint that I'd been eating jawbreakers, Mom would hit the moon. But could I see these go into the trash can? No chance! And after Dr. Mendez did his thing, I intended to do mine. I was going to chain-suck until that bag was empty.

After the meeting, I rolled up my stash and stuck it under my shirt. It was no problem sneaking it into the house past Mom. Luckily, her eyes were on the TV and not her son, who looked about as pregnant as Mrs. Bolitsky. Upstairs, I jammed the bag in a drawer and carefully arranged a week's worth of underwear over it.

One slight miscalculation. I was going to have to live with all those jawbreakers — *in my room!* — for more than two weeks. If I slipped up and took a taste — even licked a square millimeter on the lowliest B.B. Ball — I knew I wouldn't be able to stop until there wasn't a single one left!

I had to be good. And I wasn't very good at being good.

I don't know how I got any sleep at all that night.

I swear my underwear drawer was glowing. Oh, I know it wasn't *really*. But just the thought that all those jawbreakers were in there, and I could have one, two, five, a hundred — it was killing me.

And the longer I lay awake, the more my mind wandered to my conversation with Mrs. Spiro yesterday. I was even more frustrated than before. She wouldn't let me publish my article for the *Gazette*, just because it exposed Mr. Feldman's meanness — not to mention his private phone number. So the league was going to get away with this big rip-off without a single protest.

Freedom of the press — hah!

I set my jaw. Sure, Chipmunk Adelman, *student*, had to listen to Mrs. Spiro. But I was a reporter first and a student second.

But how could I ever sneak my article past her? She always read the whole paper before giving me the go-ahead to start printing. Too bad I couldn't afford to hire a hypnotist to make her think my article was just an innocent list of hockey scores and highlights. How else could I pull this off?

And suddenly I had the answer.

║║║║║ *Chapter 11*

The next morning, while I was dressing, the phone rang. I guess I picked it up at the exact same instant my mom did, because she had no idea I was on the extension.

Now, I didn't mean to eavesdrop, but it's kind of a reporter's instinct to listen in. What can I tell you? My ears have a nose for news.

"Hello, Mrs. Adelman? This is Dr. Mendez."

The dentist!

"Mrs. Adelman, I don't mean to interfere, but there's something I think you should know. I have a patient who told me she gave your son a shopping bag full of jawbreakers."

I nearly dropped the phone. Everybody else had a dentist who just fixed teeth; mine was Sherlock Holmes.

I sprang into action. I whipped those jawbreakers out of the underwear drawer, dumped them onto my bed, and wrapped the blanket around them. Then I yanked the shoelace out of my right sneaker, tied up the bundle, and threw it out the window.

I scrambled into the rest of my clothes, went downstairs, and tried to finesse my way out of the house.

"Cla-*rence*!"

You'll never believe it. She *searched* me! First she patted me down all over. Then she riffled through my backpack like a border guard. My own mother! If I wasn't totally guilty, I would have been really insulted!

Then she looked me straight in the eye and said, "Clarence, is there anything you need to tell me?"

I played it cool. "Big day at school. We're printing the new *Gazette* this morning."

She let me go. But as I went out the door, I could see her heading upstairs to ransack my room.

I darted around to the backyard and picked up my bundle of jawbreakers. I was pretty proud of my quick thinking. If I hadn't gotten those babies out of the house, they would have been dust!

I made the school bus by the skin of my teeth. And this was no day to be late. I had a lot of work to do if I wanted to get the *Gazette* out on time.

At school, I ran straight to my locker and stuffed my blanket bundle inside. Then I marched to the computer lab, powered up a word processor, and began to type.

PLAYOFFS BEGIN

by Clarence "Chipmunk" Adelman,
Gazette Sports Reporter

Last weekend was the first round of playoffs in the Waterloo Slapshot League . . .

I gave the winners. I gave the scores. I spelled out the matchups for the semifinals next Saturday. And that was it.

I took the finished article straight to Mrs. Spiro.

She smiled at me. "Clarence, I must say I'm very impressed. This shows a lot of maturity. You have my permission to start printing."

"Thank you," I said gravely.

I marched straight up to the *Gazette* office. The diskette with the rest of the paper was sitting right beside the computer keyboard.

I took the new article and ripped it into a hundred pieces. Then I pulled out the *real* article — the one blasting Mr. Feldman — and added it to the others.

Mrs. Spiro would never know who did it. Well, actually, she probably could figure it out. But by then, the *Gazette* would be printed, and everyone would already have a copy.

It was a great plan, a bold plan, a plan worthy of a true reporter. And it would have worked, too, if she hadn't walked in on me just when the first few pages were sliding out of the Copymax machine.

It took about half a second for her eyes to zero in on Mr. Feldman's unlisted phone number. I guess boldface type was a bad idea.

I expected her to start yelling. Instead, she just said, "Please leave this office, Clarence."

"But Mrs. Spiro —"

"I told you we weren't going to print your article," she said sternly. "You deliberately disobeyed me. I've looked the other way on a lot of your nonsense, Clarence, but this is the end. You no longer work for the Waterloo Elementary School *Gazette*. You're off the paper."

I felt like I'd just taken a punch in the stomach from the heavyweight champion of the world. I mean, being a reporter is more than what I do; it's who I am. If I couldn't be a reporter anymore, I couldn't be Chipmunk Adelman.

I walked out of the *Gazette* office, a stranger to myself.

||||| _Chapter 12_

I didn't have the guts to tell the team that I was off the paper. I brought my tape recorder to the semifinal on Saturday. Oh, sure, I made notes, I "recorded" the crowd noise. I even let Jared pester me into interviewing the Zamboni driver on ice maintenance. But there was no cassette in there and no batteries. My tape machine was as empty as I felt inside. Chipmunk Adelman, reporter, was a thing of the past.

The team had been driving me crazy for a couple of days. It was still going on.

"Hey, Chipmunk," called Trent, "how come the _Gazette_ has no sports section this month?"

"There wasn't any space," I lied.

"What do you mean?" he shot back. "There was a whole empty page at the back."

Luckily, I never had to answer because Trent was

73

called to center ice for the opening face-off. But I could see Alexia watching me, a curious look on her face.

The Stars' opponents were the Jolly Roger Seafood Sharks, the second-best team in the league. They had only lost three games all season, and two of those were to the Penguins. They did everything well. They had good checkers, strong skaters, rock-solid defensemen, and a stand-up goalie. They were feared around the league, but also respected. They were great guys.

And there weren't any loudmouths like Happer Feldman or Willis Gerard. Well, actually, there was one, but he wasn't a player. Roger Dinkel, owner of Jolly Roger Seafood, was the team sponsor, and he was really into his team. So for every game, he dressed himself up in a shark costume and jumped up and down on his seat, screaming his lungs out.

"Come on, Sharks, skate! These guys stink, you're gonna kill 'em! Sho-o-o-ot, no goalie out there! What are you, blind, ref? That was offside! Knock 'em on their butts. . . !"

You get the picture. He was as obnoxious as a fan could be, with his big fat head sticking out of the shark's mouth and his fin waving in the face of the guy behind him.

"Hey, look at that whosis!" Boom Boom grinned.

That was the problem. The Stars *were* looking at Jolly Roger Dinkel — instead of playing hockey. Remember, these were the Sharks — an offensive machine. They knew how to take advantage of opponents who let themselves get distracted. In no time at all, Jolly Roger Seafood jumped out to a 2–0 lead.

Boom Boom was furious. "You're getting beaten by a guy who isn't even on the thingamajig!" he raged. "Keep your minds on the whatsit!"

"We will, Coach," promised Trent.

At that moment, Jolly Roger let out a scream like a steamboat whistle. Cal laughed so hard that the Sharks' winger stole the puck from him as easily as taking candy from a baby.

Pow! Josh had to be sharp to stop the quick snap shot.

The Stars tried. They really did. But who can concentrate on hockey while somebody's screaming, *"You're Sharks, the killers of the deep! These guys are like fish sticks and crab cakes and shrimp étouffée!"*

The guy was like a sideshow clown! The Stars were still chuckling as they clattered into the locker room for the first intermission.

"Well, this is one fine thingamabob!" Boom Boom raved. The praying-mantis eyes panned across his shamefaced team and came to rest on his newest player. "Virgil — what happened? You're supposed to be bringing up the dingus!"

"The puck!" translated Alexia.

Fragile looked mystified. "You mean *now*?"

Boom Boom blew his bald dome. "Of course, *now*! This is the *playoffs*! If it doesn't happen now, it isn't going to happen at all!"

"Don't you remember all that practice?" Trent added patiently.

"Sure I do," replied Virgil. "But I didn't think you meant for me to do it in a *game*!"

By this time, Boom Boom was pulling out what was left of his hair. "When did you expect to do it? At a wedding?"

So, in the second period, the little guy did it just like in practice. Josh deflected a rebound in his direction, and Virgil began to plod up the right wing, short legs pumping. He looked so helpless, so non-dangerous, that the Sharks didn't even try to check him. Before you knew it, he was crossing the red line with a full head of steam — which, from him, was pretty pathetic.

"*Come on, Sharks!*" bellowed Jolly Roger. "*This guy can't even skate! Hit him!*"

Three in a row tried. One tripped on him; one missed completely; and the third almost killed himself flipping over the boards into the crowd.

And there were the Stars with a three-on-two rush.

Trent banged his stick on the ice. "I'm open!"

Virgil looked completely blank. He remembered the part about bringing up the puck, but we hadn't practiced passing yet.

Finally, Jared swooped in on his own player. "Give me the puck!"

"But Coach said —"

"Give me the puck!!"

Jared fed Trent, who crossed the blue line with one man to beat. Trent raised his stick to fake a slapshot, then roared around the defenseman like he wasn't even there. He made a beautiful deke and popped the puck into the top corner of the net.

"The Stars Get on the Board!" I shrieked out my headline before I realized I didn't need one. I was only an ex-reporter.

But the Stars fans were going nuts, so I tried to get into the spirit of this big moment. After all, reporter or not, I was still their number-one fan.

And what did Fragile have to say about his first assist?

"I'm sorry. I forgot to pass. I always ruin everything."

But he seemed pleased when Boom Boom gave him a big hug.

Our coach flashed the signal for a line change, but Alexia talked him into leaving Virgil on the ice with the second unit.

"He's got them running around in circles, Coach," she argued. "Let's make the most of it while they're still confused."

"Good whatsit," Boom Boom agreed.

And it paid off. Virgil teamed up perfectly with Mike Mozak. Mike was so slow that he and Virgil came chugging across the red line neck and neck, like two turtles in a race.

"*Check-check-check!*" yowled Jolly Roger.

Before we knew it, there were Sharks lying all over the ice. Virgil got the puck to Mike, who drew it way back for one of his famous shovel shots. With a sweeping motion, like a guy shoveling snow, Mike let it fly. The puck sizzled along the ice, hit the inside of the goalpost, and caromed the right way.

Tie score, 2–2. The Stars were taking over.

They forced the play into the Sharks' end, with Brian and Kyle patrolling the blue line like sentries. The passing was crisp and controlled. Shot after shot was fired at the Sharks' netminder.

Then Jolly Roger Dinkel opened up his yap again. "*What's the problem, Sharks? How can you let these wimps push you around? They're nothing but shark bait! They're not fit to carry your fins into the arena!*"

Well, even Boom Boom laughed. And once the laughing started, there was no stopping it. Cal was so hysterical that he fell down. No one touched him. He just kind of keeled over on the spot. His flailing stick tripped Kyle. With our best backward skater out of the picture, the Sharks' captain came streaking down the ice.

"Get him, Brian!" I cheered.

Our speedy defenseman overtook him from behind, tying up the puck with a stick check. But just when I thought we were safe, their captain wheeled around and kicked a beautiful drop pass to his winger who was trailing on the play.

Pow! The booming slapshot came so fast that Josh never had a chance to react. 3–2, Sharks. That was still the score when the second period ended.

The Stars were pretty deflated in the locker room.

"It's not our fault, Coach," complained Cal. "It's that sponsor of theirs. Who can concentrate on hockey when he's acting like an idiot?"

"It's not fair," agreed Jared. "The referee should call a bench penalty on the Sharks if he doesn't shut up."

Boom Boom wasn't the kind of coach who had a lot of patience for whining. Hey, the way his career went, he could have whined an opera. But every time he got sent down to the minors, he always kept on smiling with however many teeth he had left at that time.

"Come on, guys," he urged. "There's no excuse for playing like a doohickey just because some whosis in the audience is wearing a whatchamacallit suit."

"It's not just the suit, Coach," complained Kyle, defogging his rearview mirror with a piece of toilet paper. "It's what he says. He's making us laugh!"

"No crime in that," insisted Boom Boom.

"But what if he's doing it on purpose?"

I leaned over to Alexia. "I know the coach is right, but I kind of feel sorry for the players. It can't be easy to concentrate on hockey with Jolly Roger shouting the place down. Just the sight of him jumping around in that stupid costume —"

Suddenly, she interrupted me. "Chipmunk, why didn't you tell us you were kicked off the paper?"

I was so shocked that I couldn't even breathe for a minute. But I played it cool. "Why would you think something like that?"

She pointed to my tape machine. "How could you be recording when the reels aren't turning? No batteries, right?"

"Maybe I just ran out," I replied defensively.

"Chipmunk, this is me you're talking to. I've never seen you at a game without at least six spares clanking in your pockets and an extra up your nose.

You're so full of batteries that every time you burp, your eyes light up. The Energizer Bunny follows *you*. Out of batteries? I don't think so."

What could I do? I spilled my guts. "I wrote an article blasting the league for keeping you out of the playoffs. Mrs. Spiro wouldn't let me print it, and I tried to do it anyway."

Her sympathy warmed my heart. "That was pretty stupid, Chipmunk. You're a very dumb guy."

"Don't tell anybody," I pleaded. "In order to be a team reporter, you have to be — you know — a reporter."

"Don't worry," she soothed. "Just stop waving around that tape recorder. The power light isn't even on."

Sheepishly, I stuck it in my back pocket. "I guess we've got something in common," I said. "We're both victims of injustice. I'm off the paper, and you're out of the playoffs."

She looked impatient. "If you're planning to sit around feeling sorry for yourself, don't make me your partner. Now, are you going to help me get rid of Jolly Roger, or what?"

I almost swallowed my tongue. "Get *rid* of him? How?" I looked at her in disbelief. "You're not planning to, like, *mug* him, or anything like that?"

"Mug him?" It came in reverse volume control.

"We're helping the guy out. Think how cold he must get sitting so close to the ice for a whole game."

"Yeah, right!" I snorted with a laugh. "It must be a million degrees inside that shark suit! He sweats like a plow horse at the equator!"

"He's cold," she insisted. "And we're going to do everything we can to warm him up a little."

|||||| Chapter 13

To keep the fans from freezing, the rink was ringed with portable space heaters, which were pointed up at the bleachers. It was easy to find one without any people around — most of the spectators hit the snack bar between periods.

Luckily, the thing had handles, because the radiator part was burning hot. As we walked with it, I could feel my skin starting to crisp. It was a furnace!

"Hey, where are you kids going with that?"

I looked up to see one of Mr. Feldman's league vice presidents eyeing us.

"It's for the Stars," Alexia explained sweetly. "Coach Bolitsky's bald spot has been getting a little chilly."

And he let us go. We took the heater to the team bench.

"Now what?" I whispered.

No sooner were the words out of my mouth than Roger Dinkel headed to the drinking fountain, tiptoeing on his tail fins. In order to get his face down to the water, he had to pull the shark's snout back with one hand while bending himself like a pretzel over the spout. We would never have a better chance than this.

We placed the heater on the cement below the bleachers and slid it along until it was directly under Jolly Roger's seat.

Alexia cranked the knob up to maximum. "We want him toasty warm," she told me smugly.

The horn sounded, and the two teams returned to skate their warm-ups. In a few minutes, the fans had all returned, and the bleachers were packed again.

I kept a nervous eye on Jolly Roger. By this time, I was sweating like I was in a shark suit too.

The action started out fast and furious. It was obvious that the two teams had kicked into high gear for the final period. It was a classic *Sports Illustrated* setup — a one-goal game, where the winner advances to the finals and the loser goes home.

"Come on, Sharks! Go into a feeding frenzy! It's time for a shark attack!" Jolly Roger stopped jumping for a few seconds and commented, "Is it getting hot in here, or is it just me?"

It was a fantastic period of hockey, with great scoring chances for both sides and some fabulous defense. But, to be honest, I saw very little of it. I couldn't keep my eyes off Roger Dinkel. His head was hanging out of the shark's mouth. His hair was matted with sweat. And his face was the color of an overripe tomato. It must have been like a sauna in that spot, because people were edging themselves away from the Sharks' sponsor, until he found himself at the center of an empty circle of bleachers.

He was even louder and more obnoxious than before. *"There's blood in the water, Sharks! Move in for the kill! Eat 'em raw!"*

I turned to Alexia. "Your plan isn't working. The hotter he gets, the more he has to say!"

She was serene. "Patience, Chipmunk."

It happened with five minutes to go in the game. Jared was in the penalty box for tripping, so the Sharks were on the power play. If they scored and opened up their lead to 4–2, it would all be over. The Stars would never come back in a tight defensive game like this one. Well, Jolly Roger was going bananas, leaping around like a gazelle. And sweat? The guy was a fountain.

Then, right in midleap, he fainted.

At least, I thought that's what must have happened. I only looked down for a second to watch

Josh handle a tricky backhand. And when I looked back, the Sharks' sponsor was *gone*! That is, the suit was still there, but he didn't seem to be in it. I guess he just collapsed into the body of the shark. Either that or he melted like the Wicked Witch of the West.

Mr. Feldman stopped the game and sent for an ambulance. There were some pretty tense moments. Nobody could find Jolly Roger in all that costume. The paramedics finally had to pry him out of there with the "Jaws of Life" — you know, that giant contraption they use to cut into car wrecks.

I knew there was a fantastic headline in there somewhere — about using jaws to get a guy out of a shark. But I couldn't nail it down.

And that awful Jolly Roger! The minute he came to, he yelled right in the ambulance driver's face, *"Come on, Sharks! Chew 'em up and spit 'em out!"*

The guy didn't miss a beat. He just kept on cheering like he didn't notice that everything had come to a halt so he could receive emergency medical attention. Man, did he kick up a fuss when they told him he had to go to the hospital so they could make sure he was really okay.

He got a roar of applause when he left the building. I'll bet most of the crowd was happy because his big mouth was going with him.

Finally, the game resumed. With Jolly Roger gone,

there were no more excuses for the Stars. It was fish or cut bait.

I guess you couldn't blame the Sharks for a little confusion after the collapse of their sponsor. The Stars got some great rushes, both with Virgil and with Kyle's backward attack. These led to some dangerous scoring chances, but the Sharks' goalie always seemed to come up with the clutch saves.

Then, with less than two minutes to play, Trent got his stick on the puck just inside the Sharks' blue line. I don't know what made him decide not to skate with it. He was normally such a finesse player, with so many great moves. But whatever the reason, he just wheeled and unloaded a booming slapshot.

Somehow the puck managed to find its way through a sea of arms, legs, and sticks in front of the Sharks' net. Their goalie reached for it with his blocker, but he was too late.

"All tied up!" I howled as the Mars fans erupted into celebration.

Now it was anybody's game. The Stars and the Sharks pulled out all the stops and turned the pressure up to an unbearable level. It was an even contest, but I had to give a slight advantage to Mars Health Food. As a good team, the Sharks usually didn't need last-second heroics. But the Stars had been scrambling from behind since day one of the team's existence. They were used to having their backs against the wall. But could they do it again?

Coach Bolitsky decided to go back to the plan that had been the most successful so far.

"Give it to Whatsisname!" he bellowed.

"Virgil!" translated Alexia.

And the little guy did great. He seemed to be going a bit faster this time. He even remembered that he had to pass.

I stared in horror. Our dweeb put the puck right on the stick of the Sharks' captain!

From out of nowhere dove Trent Ruben. He hurled himself at the captain just as the kid brought his stick forward for a blistering drive.

Wham! Checker and checkee went flying. The puck trickled harmlessly in to Josh. But our goalie didn't want it anywhere near his net. He golfed a clearing pass all the way to the neutral zone.

Bonk! It hit Cal right in the face mask. The impact was so hard that our big winger dropped like a stone. When he scrambled to his feet, half the community center was screaming at him.

"Go, Cal!" I howled. *"You've got a breakaway!"*

Now, Cal was no speedster. But he had a ten-foot lead over the nearest Sharks' defenseman. He came roaring in on goal and took the worst shot I've ever seen — right into the goalie's pads!

"No-o-o-o!" wailed Boom Boom.

But the best thing about Cal was that he never gave up. He hacked at the rebound and swung at the second rebound.

"It's between your doohickeys!" cried the coach.

"Your skates!" I translated.

Still fighting, Cal kicked the puck up to his stick and knocked it under the goalie's glove and into the net.

4–3, Stars. Exactly five seconds remained on the clock. It just wasn't enough time for the Sharks to get anything going. The buzzer sounded.

The Stars from Mars — the team nobody wanted, the joke of the league — were going to the finals. Miracle.

The locker room was bedlam. The players were so pumped they didn't even mind that Mrs. B. was handing out cabbage and tofu wraps while she devoured an extra-large Philadelphia cheese steak. Cal hadn't stopped screaming since his goal. Even Virgil looked kind of happy.

It was so loud in there that I didn't get a chance to talk to Alexia until we were riding home in the Mars Health Food van.

"Hey," I whispered. "When we put that heater under Jolly Roger's seat, you didn't know the guy was going to wind up in the hospital, right?"

She shot me a dazzling smile. "Whatever you say, Chipmunk."

I'm glad Alexia Colwin is my friend. Because if she was my enemy, I don't think I'd sleep another night for the rest of my life.

||||| *Chapter 14*

On Monday morning, I was on my way out the door when my mother announced that she needed to talk to me.

That was never a good sign. "Sorry, Mom. I'm late for the bus."

"This won't take long," she insisted. "Clarence, I have a confession to make. I was so sure that you had Mrs. Bolitsky's jawbreakers that I actually searched your room."

I was amazed. She was blushing with embarrassment.

"I know now that I should have believed you," she went on, "and I'm sorry."

What could I do? I forgave her. It was easy, especially since I knew that Mrs. B.'s jawbreakers were safely wrapped in my blue blanket, stuffed into my locker at school.

"I hope you've learned a valuable lesson about trust, Mom," I couldn't resist adding. Hey, it was a little sleazy, but she didn't know that.

"I'll try, Clarence. Oh, incidentally, I can't seem to find your blue blanket."

I resumed my run for the door. "Maybe it's in the laundry," I tossed over my shoulder. Or in my locker, filled with jawbreakers.

The school bus was a party on wheels. Just the thought that the Mars Health Food Stars would be playing for the Feldman Cup was blowing everybody away. We were going to lose, of course. Our opponents — big surprise — were the Powerhouse Penguins, who had creamed the Red Wings 11–zip in the game after ours.

Josh gave a contented sigh. "As far as I'm concerned, Saturday was *our* championship. I mean, we didn't win it all, but we sure showed Waterloo that we belong in their league."

Brian nodded. "We did everything we set out to do this year."

"Except drive the Zamboni," Jared said wistfully.

"Still, it would be nice to make a good showing against the Penguins," Cal added.

Alexia was totally disgusted, which meant we

could hardly hear her. "Would you idiots at least wait for the opening face-off before you surrender?"

"Come on, Lex," her brother chided. "You know we haven't got a chance against the Penguins."

"We beat them once," Alexia pointed out.

"That was a flukey win on our bumpy rink in Mars," Josh reminded her. "Flukes don't happen in the finals. It's a two-game series — total goals. We're without our captain. And the Penguins are better than ever. Happer Feldman has nine goals in two rounds of playoffs! Sure, let's think positive. But let's not lie to ourselves."

"Ask Chipmunk," Kyle suggested. "Reporters have to be honest." Our backward-skating defenseman turned to face me. "If the *Gazette* was coming out today, would you put that we have a chance against the Penguins?"

I tried to make a joke out of it. "Well, Fragile went a whole game without bleeding on anybody. So there's no limit to what might happen for the Stars."

It broke the mood. The Stars and their classmates from Mars laughed all the way to school.

I knew something was up the second I walked into the building. There was a nervous buzz in the hall. I pulled aside the first kid I saw. "What's up?"

"Locker inspection," he replied. "Mr. Lambert's searching the whole seven-hundred hall."

"Seven hundred? But that's *my* hallway!" I was so horrified that I didn't even ask what the principal was looking for. I was too worried about what he was going to find.

You're probably wondering what the big deal was. I mean, there's no law against having a few hundred jawbreakers in a school locker. But back when I first got those eleven cavities, my mom told the whole world about it. She even wrote a letter for the bulletin board in the teachers' lounge. You'd have to be a cave-dwelling hermit not to know that I was living under dental martial law. When Mr. Lambert cracked my locker and saw all those jawbreakers, he was going to call my mother for sure. Maybe it hadn't been such a good idea to give Mom that lecture about trust.

I melted into the group of students that ringed Mr. Lambert and our custodian, Mr. Sarkis. The principal didn't exactly uncover a crime wave. Sure, one kid had a library book from 1996; another guy had a picture of a movie star wearing a bathing suit the size of a postage stamp; the girl with the six-month-old piece of pizza got a lecture, but no detention. And then it was my turn.

"What's this — a bedspread?" As the custodian

pulled out my blue blanket, I closed my eyes and waited for the rat-a-tat of hundreds of jawbreakers hitting the terrazzo floor.

It didn't come.

"I've been robbed!" I blurted out. "I mean —"

The principal and the custodian held up my blanket between them. I couldn't believe it. It must have been the dampness in the school or something. Every single one of Mrs. Bolitsky's jawbreakers was now stuck to that blanket.

The principal's eyes narrowed. "Clarence, what is this?"

I started to sweat. "It's a — it's a —"

"It's a star map of the Milky Way galaxy," came a voice from behind me.

I wheeled. There stood little Virgil Knox, examining my blanket with interest.

"A star map?" frowned Mr. Sarkis.

"We're doing astronomy in Mr. Ping's class," Fragile explained. He turned to me. "Where did you get the idea to do a star map for science?"

"I thought it would be — uh — uh —" I searched my mind and came up empty. "— scientific."

The principal raised an eyebrow. For a minute there I almost thought he bought it. But then who should come walking down the hall but Mr. Ping himself. My luck.

Mr. Lambert held out my blanket. "Does this look like a galaxy to you?"

My breath caught in my throat. This was the end.

"As a matter of fact it does," the science teacher said in a pleased tone. "Note the larger concentration of stars toward the center, with the sparser spiral arms at the edges."

Well, what do you know? Galaxies are laid out exactly the same way jawbreakers stick to a blanket. You learn something new every day.

Mr. Ping seemed impressed. "And the different colored balls represent the various types of stars in our galaxy. Very creative. Clarence, is this your work?"

I nodded. "But I guess I'd better take it home to — uh — finish it off."

"Absolutely not," said Mr. Ping. "This has to go up where the whole school can see it."

"Let's hang it in the cafeteria," suggested Mr. Lambert.

If you had a stockpile of jawbreakers, would you put it in a room with eight hundred hungry kids? "Make sure you hang it really high," I pleaded. "You wouldn't want anybody to, you know, eat any of the Milky Way galaxy."

For some reason, all the adults thought that was really hilarious.

When the bell rang, I turned to Virgil to thank him for saving my life. But the little guy had already run off to class. To this day I don't know if he said what he did out of team loyalty. Or maybe he honestly looks at jawbreakers stuck to a blanket and sees a galaxy.

Chapter 15 \\\\\\

The Stars weren't exactly favored to beat the Penguins in the finals. The word around town was that most people thought we weren't going to get a single goal in the entire two-game playoff. Powerhouse Gas and Electric, the Penguins' sponsor, had already printed up championship T-shirts. Naturally, these weren't supposed to be handed out until after the weekend. But guess who got his hands on one early and had the nerve to wear it to school: Happer Feldman.

He wore it as an undershirt. So whenever there were any adults around, it was covered up. But he flashed it at us Marsers every chance he got. If you look up "jerkface" in the dictionary, you'll probably find a picture of Happer.

"You've got a two-game series to play before you

can wear that shirt," I snarled at him. "And you can't be a hundred percent sure you're going to win."

"I can't be a hundred percent sure the sun's going to come up tomorrow either," he laughed. "It's like I said before. No Martian will ever lay his — or *her* — alien finger on the Feldman Cup."

As if on cue, Alexia walked into class. Happer leaped up on a chair and puffed out his chest, sticking the victory T-shirt right in her face.

I was proud of her. She looked through him like he wasn't even there.

The big idiot followed her to her seat. "What do you think of my T-shirt?"

"I think it might be worth a lot of money when the Stars beat you," was her bland reply.

"Beat us?" Happer crowed. "The way I've been playing, I could beat you Martians by myself!"

"I'll bet you'd like that," Alexia commented. "Too bad there are all those other morons on your team. Him, for one." She was pointing at Oliver Witt.

It was usually pretty easy for Alexia to goad those two dummies into a rage. But not today. That's how I knew the Penguins were extremely confident about the weekend series.

And not just the team. The whole city of Waterloo was very sure that the Penguins wouldn't have to do much more than show up to win their third straight championship. Why, when the Waterloo newspaper did an article on the Slapshot League finals, they didn't even bother mentioning who the Penguins' opponents were going to be. It used to drive me nuts when they called us Martians and space hicks and cosmo-nuts. But maybe that was better than being totally ignored.

Boom Boom was worried about how his team would react to all this. "Just because people treat you like doohickeys doesn't mean you're not who-sises!" he roared.

It could have meant a lot of things. But it was probably encouragement for the Stars not to count themselves out just because everybody else did.

"Where have *you* been, Chipmunk?" complained Brian. "Our team reporter should be sticking up for us when nobody else will!"

And, man, did I feel terrible about that! It was like I was letting everybody down.

Alexia came to my rescue. "Lay off Chipmunk," she ordered. "It's not his fault the *Gazette* always comes out at the wrong time."

I was grateful for her support. But it just made me feel worse to remember that I was unemployed.

When the Stars met at Mars Health Food before game one of the finals, they were as nervous as a procession of prisoners on their way to the electric chair. Who wouldn't be? I was freaking out, and I didn't even have to put on a pair of skates.

And if we were nuts, how about Virgil? He saw the finals as a chance to make the whole town hate him, not just the Stars. But I've got to give him credit. He was trying. He even came to Mars for the team breakfast. Man, you should have seen his face when he took his first bite of tofu waffles with soybean hash. He looked like someone had just piped his pants full of ice water. I'm sure he wanted to say something or, at the very least, spit it out. But the rest of us were such experts at pretending we liked it that I guess he figured he'd better keep quiet.

Believe me, it wasn't easy for any of us to choke down soybean hash while watching Mrs. B. take apart a cream-filled chocolate-covered bearclaw that was at least a foot long.

Speaking of Mrs. B., our coach's wife was getting bigger every day. I knew the most beautiful lady in the world was in there somewhere, but right now she was a tank. The baby wasn't due for a couple of months, which was kind of a scary thought. I've heard that pregnant women get biggest at the very end. By June, our Mrs. B. would be getting her own area code from the phone company.

After breakfast, Boom Boom made a speech that

was ninety percent whatchamacallits and doohickeys. Mrs. B. translated, but her mouth was so full of pastry that we didn't get much of that either.

"That's exactly what I meant," our coach confirmed. He slapped his knee. "All right, everybody into the thingamabob. Let's get this show on the whatsit."

So the Stars headed for their date with destiny propelled by great wisdom. Too bad they didn't understand any of it.

"He's proud of us," Alexia whispered when we were all crammed into the health food van.

"He said that?" asked Virgil, wide-eyed.

She nodded seriously. "I've been learning to speak doohickey."

Someone must have messed with the sign over the big doors of the community center. When Coach Bolitsky opened the back of the truck, we were greeted by the message:

SLAPSHOT LEAGUE FINAL: PENGUINS VS. RATSS

Cal thought that was hilarious — especially when Virgil said, "I thought *we* were playing in the finals. Who are the Ratss?"

We stepped through the doors and froze. It was enough to wipe the smirk off even Cal's face. The arena was like Madison Square Garden. Extra portable bleachers had been wheeled into every open space around the rink. There must have been seating for two thousand in there.

Trent took a deep breath. "Finals hockey. People who don't know a puck from a doorknob show up for these games."

Josh looked around. "But where are *our* fans?"

It was what we were all thinking. It seemed like every single seat was filled by a Waterloo type.

It took a little searching, but we located some Marsers. They were sprinkled about the back rows and stairs of the bleachers and peering through the cloudy glass of the snack bar. Even pregnant Mrs. B. had to stand, jammed in with my mom and a few other parents beside the Zamboni. They were so tightly packed that there was barely enough room for the coach's wife's bag of peanut butter cookies.

"We'll tell our folks to come earlier tomorrow," Alexia decided. "They'll want better seats for when we win it all."

Josh frowned at her. "I hope you're kidding, Lex."

"Do I look like I'm kidding?" she countered.

The skull and crossbones on a poison label looked more like it was kidding than Alexia Colwin. Was she nuts? The Penguins seemed unbeatable. They had the best players, the top coach, the most fans.

Even their uniforms were nicer than everybody else's. This crowd wasn't here to watch a hockey game. They were here to see the Penguins kill us.

On the other hand, we had Boom Boom. He wasn't exactly Gordie Howe. But he *did* play in the NHL. And he had a couple of secret weapons up his sleeve.

He tried weapon number one on the very first play of the game. Trent won the face-off and got the puck to Fragile, who began his slow, plodding "rush" up ice. I was on the bench with the team — who could find a seat in that mob scene? We all stood up for a better view. Nobody wanted to miss the sight of Happer and Oliver trying to check Virgil and landing flat on their faces.

But it didn't happen. Instead, Happer, Oliver, and their center, Gavin Avery, formed a half-circle around the puck carrier, blocking his passing lanes.

"We've been scouting you Martians!" Happer sneered as he passed our bench. "Your cheap tricks aren't going to work anymore!"

They shadowed Virgil the full length of the rink.

"He's running out of skating room!" I exclaimed.

"Sho-o-o-ot!" bellowed Boom Boom.

But this was Virgil. He had only practiced passing. No one had told him anything about shooting.

"Hey," said Cal, fascinated, "you don't suppose he'll just keep on going, do you?"

"Of course not," snapped Alexia. "Nobody could be *that* stupid."

Crash! Virgil's body went into the boards, his face mask hit the glass, and you can guess the rest. Picture Niagara Falls in valentine red.

Chapter 16 \ \ \ \ \ \

Gasps of shock and even some screams went up in the bleachers. I mean, the spectators didn't know Fragile as well as we did. But the officials kept everybody calm while Virgil got the flood stopped up. The only big delay came when Jared offered the Zamboni driver ten dollars to let him do the cleanup, and the guy looked like he was going to say yes. The driver bargained Jared up to thirty-five bucks before Mr. Feldman came over and ordered the man to get on with his job or else.

Our winger was not so easily put off. "If he gets fired," Jared wheedled, "can I drive the Zamboni until you hire a replacement?"

Mr. Feldman blew his stack. "Get back to the bench or I'll call a penalty on the Stars!"

Jared was sulky. "That Mr. Feldman," he moped to the team. "He always ruins everything!"

When play finally resumed, Boom Boom played his other trump card, Kyle's reverse attack.

Kyle was tough to check, since he always had his back to you, almost like a basketball point guard protecting his dribble. Thanks to his rearview mirror, he knew where all the defenders were, and also his own teammates if he wanted to pass.

But Coach Monahan of the Penguins was pretty sharp. He'd figured out how to stop Virgil, and he had a plan for Kyle as well.

Instead of trying to hit Kyle, Oliver dove between his legs, poke-checking the puck to Gavin. Gavin head-manned a pass over center to Happer, who had a breakaway.

Happer came roaring in on goal all alone. He drew the puck back ever so slightly. Then, with a lightning-quick flick of his wrists, he fired it into the net behind Josh.

When two thousand people go nuts in a small arena, the individual cheers meld together into a thunderous roar.

"Nice whatchamacallit," Coach Bolitsky admitted ruefully. He had to shout to be heard over the Penguins fans.

"Too nice," I agreed grimly.

Naturally, Happer couldn't keep his celebration to himself. "Wayne Gretzky's hockey clinic!" He grinned, waving his stick at the Stars' bench.

"You're nothing special!" Cal hollered back. To us, he whispered, "You think Wayne Gretzky really taught him how to shoot like that?"

"It was a fluke," exclaimed Alexia. "He couldn't do it again in a million years."

Actually, it took about three minutes. Cal was in the penalty box for hooking, so the Penguins had a power play. Oliver outmuscled Brian in the corner and made a perfect pass to Happer in the slot. Happer stopped the puck and *pow*! It was that wrist shot again. Josh never had a chance. As quick as that, the Stars found themselves in a 2–0 hole. Presto — instant disaster.

Don't get me wrong. I'd seen the Stars losing before. But all those other times, I could see them skating badly, making mistakes, and playing sloppily. Today they were really hustling out there. After each shift, they'd come to the bench winded and gasping. That was the scary part. It's easy to improve on a lousy effort. All you have to do is play harder. But when you're doing your absolute best and still getting massacred, it's hopeless.

Happer sewed up his hat trick before the first period was even over. It was another wrist shot, of course, this one up high. Josh was nowhere near it.

Down 3–0, the Stars needed a defensive stand in the second period. And I have to say they put together fifteen minutes of the tightest-checking hockey I've ever seen. Happer couldn't touch the puck without Trent or Cal in his face. Brian and Kyle were awesome, blocking drives and keeping the Penguin forwards away from the net. After allowing eighteen shots on goal in the first period, the Stars held the Penguins to only three shots in the second — none of them from Happer Feldman.

"Where's your wrist shot now?" Cal blustered to Happer.

The league president's nephew laughed. "You're playing perfect hockey — *if* you were protecting a lead. The only problem is you're down three goals, *Einstein!*"

He had a point. Mars Health Food had stymied the Penguins — but the Stars weren't scoring either. And *we* were the ones trying to come from behind.

In the third period Coach Bolitsky had no choice but to pull the plug on the defensive game and try to get some offense going. The first headline idea that popped into my head was *Bold Move*, but I had to revise it to *Big Mistake*. With Trent attacking instead of shadowing Happer, it wasn't too long before the famous Wayne Gretzky wrist shot got another opportunity. Before you knew it, the puck was in the net, and Josh was flat on his face on the ice, looking like a complete clod. This time there were laughs mixed in with the roar from the Waterloo fans.

His stick raised high in celebration, Happer skated right to the scorer's box. He leaped up on the boards, stuck his face into the microphone, and bellowed, *"Mar-tians!!"*

Waves of laughter rocked the community center. Happer got chewed out by Coach Monahan and benched for one shift. But by that time, the damage was already done.

A chant of "Space hicks! Space hicks! Space hicks!" went up among the kids in the crowd. The Mars jokes were flying in fast and furious from the bleachers.

"Hey, galaxy goofballs! Is that what they call hockey on Mars?"

"I can smell your asteroid breath from here!"

"Go shovel your alien fertilizer at home!"

I should say that it wasn't the Waterloo adults yelling any of that stuff. But they sure weren't breaking their necks to shut their kids up.

I was so mad, I'm amazed I wasn't blowing smoke out my ears. The Stars hadn't been treated this badly

110

since their first game in the league. They were in the finals! They deserved more respect than this!

The players were rigid and grim-faced. Boom Boom's ponytail was standing straight up like an antenna. As for Alexia — her jaw was stuck out so far that she could have used it as a battering ram.

Then some Waterloo jerk had the *nerve* to call out, "Hey, Martians, where's your captain? Out selling Girl Scout cookies?"

Like Alexia had deserted the team, instead of being kicked off just for being a girl! Well, it got to me — the game, the league, and four months of taunts and rip-offs against Mars.

I leaped up on the bench and started screaming at the whole crowd. *"Shut up, you rotten, snobby, back-stabbing —"*

I never got to finish my string of insults. For the first time all season, Coach Boom Boom Bolitsky kicked me out of the game.

Chapter 17 \\\\\\

Well, he didn't kick me out exactly. He said, "Chipmunk, go to the gizmo," and I was pretty sure he meant the locker room. That's where I spent the rest of the Stars' thrashing.

Oh, sure, I watched the game. I was too much of a natural reporter not to poke my head out the door and take in the last few minutes of action. But when Oliver scored to bump the Penguins' lead up to 5–0, it was just too painful to watch. The Stars were trying, but they were totally outclassed. They barely belonged on the same ice as their opponents. Who knew what the score could be after tomorrow's game — 10–0? 12–0? What a lousy finish to a great Cinderella story. This would be like Cinderella dating the prince, but on her way to the wedding, she gets run over by a bus, struck by lightning, and eaten by a werewolf.

So I sat there, furious, bummed out, and kind of bored, too. Change rooms aren't exactly Disney World, you know. They're ugly, smelly places where, if you're lucky, somebody left an old newspaper or magazine to read. All I could dig up in this dump was a Sports World catalog from fall 1997. It was folded over and sticking out of one of the lockers.

Hey, anything was better than watching the slaughter on the ice. I pulled it out and started leafing through the ads for golf clubs, tennis rackets, and skis. I couldn't help scowling at the pictures of happy kids holding hockey sticks.

"Go ahead, smile," I growled at the boy on the page. "You're not on a team where you get kicked around just because of your hometown. What do you care?"

The photograph didn't answer. It kept right on grinning its message: *Hockey Sticks — Wood $19.99; Aluminum $29.99.*

The word jumped out at me — Aluminum! *Aluminum!!*

I thought back to that old 1887 law that was keeping Alexia out of the playoffs: *No female personage shall be permitted to hold, or otherwise wield, a length of wood exceeding three feet . . .*

A length of *wood*.

I leaped up, punched the air, and howled, *"Ya-hoooo!!"*

It was at that very moment that the door opened and the team dragged themselves into the locker room behind Coach Bolitsky. They must have thought I was nuts, jumping for joy while the Stars were blown out and humiliated.

Alexia scorched me with a searing look. "I *hope* you just won the lottery, Chipmunk," she said through clenched teeth. "Or have you turned into a big Happer Feldman fan?"

"You can play! You can *play!*" I pushed the catalog into her face. "With *this!*"

She gawked like she was having trouble believing her own eyes. "I can play," she said finally.

If I didn't know this was Alexia, I would have sworn I saw her blink back two big tears.

She handed the catalog to Boom Boom and the players gathered around. The praying-mantis eyes bulged even wider than usual. "A whatchamacallit doohickey!" he exclaimed.

"An aluminum stick!" Trent translated breath-lessly. "It isn't covered under that old law because it isn't a length of wood. It's a length of aluminum!"

114

"They didn't even have aluminum way back in 1887!" I added excitedly.

"We've got our captain back!" roared Cal.

It was the kind of moment that *Sports Illustrated* loves to write about: A team inspired and united, powered by high fives and hope. It was awesome — everybody cheering and babbling out pledges to chip in money to buy that aluminum stick. I was so psyched that I almost didn't notice the slight figure slinking out the door.

Alexia saw it too. "Freeze!" she barked. "Virgil, where are you going?"

Bent over by the weight of his sports bag, the poor kid was so short that his duffel looked kind of like a giant insect about to eat him. "Home," he replied.

"Home?" cried Boom Boom. "We've got our whosis back. We have to have a team thingamabob to plan our whatsit for tomorrow."

"Our strategy," I translated.

"But you've got your captain again," Fragile argued. "What do you need me for?"

The coach put an arm around his shoulder. "Because you're one of us," he said. "We're a team. We play together; we win together; we go down in dinguses together."

"Flames," supplied Trent.

"You're just going to wind up hating me," warned Virgil.

"That's a chance we're willing to take," grinned the captain of the Stars.

Game two of the Slapshot League final was scheduled for four o'clock Sunday afternoon. Believe it or not, the bleachers weren't quite as packed as they had been yesterday. After all, we were starting today with the Penguins up 5–zip, so people figured the series was over. Today's crowd was here more to see the presentation of the trophy than anything else. There were a lot of families and friends of the players, and even a few of the top brass of Powerhouse Gas and Electric.

Mars, on the other hand, had a great turnout. After our shopping trip to Sports World to buy the aluminum stick, the players and I spent the evening spreading the word that the Stars had one last trick up their sleeves. We were careful not to promise victory, of course. Down five goals, that was practically impossible. But with Alexia back, we sure planned to make those jerks work for their trophy.

Our fans came early today, so they were sitting right up front where the Stars could see them and feel their support. Good old Mrs. B. was directly behind the Stars' bench. She was saving my usual seat for me using a giant jalapeño cheese ball and a box of Ritz crackers — which wasn't really necessary. She pretty much took up two seats all by herself.

Happer and Oliver were holding court around the snack bar when the Stars arrived.

"Hey, Ruben, where's your girlfriend?" Oliver taunted Trent. "Oh, excuse me, your *captain*."

"Captain girlfriend," chuckled Happer.

They were right. Alexia was nowhere to be seen. Luckily, neither of those idiots noticed that Boom Boom and Cal were struggling with a very long, very heavy duffel bag.

Trent shrugged. "Your uncle won't let her play. I guess he doesn't think his nephew is tough enough to handle her."

"That's not it!" Happer exploded. "It's the law! We obey the laws on *Earth*."

"I'll bet she isn't here because she's sick of watching you Martians play like stiffs," added Oliver. "Some loyalty!"

"Enough of this heejazz," interrupted Coach Bolitsky. "Let's get to the thingamabob."

But even as we walked away, Happer called after us, "Was I right or was I right? No Martian is ever going to lay an alien finger on the Feldman Cup!"

In the locker room, Boom Boom unzipped the big duffel, and Alexia scrambled free and dusted herself off. Her iron jaw was already jutting out in front of her. "That Happer — what a bigmouth! Too bad the sports bag didn't have any flaps. I would have reached out and decked him."

"You'll get your chance," promised Boom Boom. "On the whatsit."

The plan was to use the element of surprise. The players would try to keep Alexia's return a secret as long as possible. She wore the Stars' spare jersey, number thirteen. We rented skates for her, since her own were white. We even replaced her clear visor with a dark-tinted one so the Penguins wouldn't get a good look at her face. Her fair hair was tucked up inside her helmet.

On the ice, the coach moved her to right defense from her usual right wing. That way, she wouldn't have to line up for the face-off opposite Happer, who might recognize her.

Trent won the draw, but Jared couldn't handle the pass, and Oliver wound up with the puck. He fed Gavin, who broke across the Stars' blue line.

Wham!

Alexia came out of nowhere and put the Penguins' center flat on his back with a beautiful shoulder check. Brian and Happer made for the loose puck. Brian was faster, but Happer got his stick in front of the clearing pass, which went high into the stands.

Happer eyed Alexia. "Who's that?"

But before he could investigate, the referee called Trent and Gavin to the dot for the next face-off.

It was just outside the Stars' zone. This time, Gavin tied Trent up and Happer poked the puck to Oliver on the left wing.

Crunch!

Alexia came clear across the ice and rammed him into the boards. She whacked a pass to Brian, who led the Stars' rush. The Penguins' goalie had to be quick to handle Jared's slapshot.

Happer still wasn't sure what was going on, but he was tattling anyway. "Coach!" he called to his bench. "They're cheating! They've got someone new!"

Coach Monahan frowned at Alexia. "Hey!" he called over the penalty box. "What are you trying to pull, Bolitsky?"

Boom Boom shrugged innocently. "Just a thinga-majig."

"A *what*?"

But by then the play had begun again. Jared had the puck in the corner, but Happer intercepted his centering pass. He came roaring over the blue line with one defender to beat — Alexia.

"I'm taking you to school, Martian," he panted, managing to sneer even though he was on an all-out rush.

He faked left, then accelerated, trying to blow by her on the right. But as he pulled around, he got a good look into her darkened visor.

His eyes bulged. "*You?*"

Chapter 18

Alexia hit him with a hip check straight out of an NHL training film. He went flying over her like a leapfrogger with a jet-propulsion backpack.

Crash!!

By the time he hit the ice, Alexia had stolen the puck and was thundering over the Penguins' blue line.

"I'm open!" called Trent.

"Not now, hotshot!" she growled. I've never heard a voice like that coming from a human throat.

Oliver tried a poke-check, and she lifted up a skate and stomped on his stick so hard that it splintered and clattered out of his hands. She just plain steamrolled the defenseman who tried to hit her.

Pow! Her shot was low and hard. It glanced off the edge of the goalie's pad and into the net.

"No More Shutout!" I howled my headline as the Mars fans roared to their feet. My tape recorder was loaded up with a new cassette and batteries. In honor of Alexia's return, I had vowed to report on this game just like I was still working for the *Gazette*.

Happer was just now picking himself back up off the ice after that monster check. "That's Alexia Colwin!" he snapped at the ref. "She's out of the league! That goal shouldn't count!"

The official turned to Alexia. "Is that true, son? I mean — you know what I mean."

In answer, Alexia pulled off her helmet. Blond hair cascaded down to her shoulders. The gasp that went up in the arena was loud enough to move the needle of the sound-level meter on my tape recorder.

"She's breaking the law!" Oliver accused. "Call the cops!"

I guess he meant the hockey stick enforcement patrol.

Naturally, Mr. Feldman had to stick his nose into it. He came over to give the official league ruling. "Since it was scored by an ineligible player, the goal is disallowed. And you, young lady," he added to Alexia, "should have some respect for the law. Put down that stick and leave the ice at once."

"But it's a whatchamacallit doohickey!" bellowed Boom Boom.

"A *what*?" Coach Monahan was really confused.

"Waterloo statutes prevent her from carrying a length of wood exceeding three feet," lectured the league president. "We may not like it, but the law's the law."

"But it's not a length of wood," Trent protested. "It's a length of *aluminum*!"

Alexia raised her foot and smacked her skate blade with her stick. The clink of metal on metal was unmistakable.

Mr. Feldman was dumbfounded. "An aluminum stick?"

"A whatchamacallit doohickey," agreed Coach Bolitsky.

"Well, this is — this is —" The league president's face twisted. "— *wonderful*."

Happer's jaw dropped. "You mean you're going to let her play?"

"Of course," his uncle beamed. "The league felt terrible about excluding a talented player like Alexia. It was only the law that made us do it."

If you swallow that, then you probably also believe in the tooth fairy. Mr. Feldman was only letting our captain in because he couldn't think of another excuse to keep her out.

Just having Alexia back changed the game. Her tough body checks made the Penguins think twice about going after loose pucks. They didn't hesitate long, but it was just enough for the Stars to get the jump on them. Pretty soon, Jared beat Oliver into the corner and feathered a perfect pass out to Trent in the slot. Our assistant captain faked a shot, then expertly pulled the puck to his backhand and popped it into the net. Now it was 5–2.

Coach Monahan used his time-out early. "What's the problem, guys?" he bawled at his unsettled team. "You're playing like a bunch of scaredy-cats out there! So their captain's back. So what? We're the *Penguins*! If we can't beat them *with* her, then we've got no right to call ourselves the best!"

It was a great speech, and the Penguins came out strong. Amazingly, the Stars stood right up to them. There was end-to-end action, with great offense for both sides. But nobody scored. Then, just before the end of the period, Happer squirmed free of a check right in front of the Stars' net. Oliver got him the puck and *pow*! It was 6–2.

"Why can't I stop that shot?" cried Josh in the locker room, pounding his pads with his goalie stick.

Trent couldn't figure it out either. "It isn't *harder* than anybody else's wrist shot."

Coach Bolitsky looked thoughtful. "It always seems like you're flopping in the wrong direction," he suggested, the praying-mantis eyes whirling in his head, "leaving that Happer whosis half the doo-jig to shoot at."

"It's Wayne Gretzky's wrist shot," put in Brian. "There's no way a mere kid can ever learn to stop it."

"It isn't Wayne Gretzky's wrist shot," Alexia explained patiently. "He may have *learned* it at Wayne Gretzky's clinic, but Happer's just a regular twelve-year-old with a bad attitude and a mouth the size of the Grand Canyon. Josh, keep trying. You'll get the better of Happer before this game is through."

Josh was smiling again as the teams returned to the ice for the second period. But it took less than a minute for Happer to get the better of Josh. It was on an all-out four-man rush that ended up with Happer on a clean breakaway. He just aimed and fired. Josh wasn't even close to making the save.

7–2, Penguins. The Stars were down five goals again. They were no better off than at the end of game one. Things got very quiet on the Stars' bench. Even Boom Boom had no comment. The only sound was the constant munch, munch, munch of Mrs. Bolitsky putting away an entire box of crackers with her jalapeño cheese ball, which was now down to a sort of cheese hemisphere.

Then, miracle of miracles, the Stars got a break. Alexia hammered Happer into the boards on a totally legal check. But Happer was so enraged that he reached out his stick and slashed at her leg as she tried to skate away. Down went our captain, and up went the referee's arm.

"Deliberate intent to injure!" the ref barked. "That's a major penalty!"

IIIII **Chapter 19**

A major penalty! This was *huge*! Majors last five minutes instead of the usual two. And they don't end if the other team scores. So the Stars would be on the power play for the whole time!

Naturally, Happer was a big crybaby about it. "No fair!" he shouted at the ref. "You only gave me the major because she's a *girl*!"

"Can it, Feldman," ordered Coach Monahan from the Penguins' bench. "You should know better than to try a cheap shot like that."

I've never seen Boom Boom so excited. He was darting around the bench so fast that his ponytail was twirling like the rotor blade of a helicopter. I thought he was nuts to send out Virgil instead of Jared on left wing. But with the Penguins a player short, they didn't have the manpower to surround him and cut off his passing lanes.

When Fragile crossed the blue line, Gavin tried a body check and wound up slamming himself into the boards. The little guy got the puck to Alexia, who found Trent for a picture-perfect tip-in.

We cheered like crazy, but the Stars' power play was only getting started. Boom Boom called time-out to rest his attackers. Two minutes later, Brian used his superspeed to lead a spectacular end-to-end rush. The Penguins' goalie made the first save, but Alexia stampeded the crease, grabbed the rebound, and managed to muscle it into the net. 7–4. And just as Happer stepped out of the penalty box, Oliver tried to flip him a breakaway pass. Kyle blocked it at the blue line and backed into the slot. In his rearview mirror, he must have been able to see the traffic jam of Penguins screening the goalie. His shot wasn't very hard, but it bounced off a couple of skate blades and dribbled into the net.

The Mars fans were going nuts. Mrs. B. hugged me, crushing what was left of her cheese ball against my jacket. I mean, this was a game again! It was 7–5!

The rest of the period turned into the toughest-checking, hardest-skating hockey I've ever seen in the Slapshot League. Fans of both teams were on their feet, screaming themselves hoarse. The Penguins were all over the ice, playing like two-time defending champions. But there were our Stars, matching them stride for stride.

Then, just before the end of the period, the Penguins struck again. Oliver poked the puck away from Cal in the corner. He danced around our winger and made a beautiful centering pass to Happer in the slot. You can guess the rest. That wrist shot — that rotten, stinking, miserable wrist shot! How could Wayne Gretzky teach it to a total jerk like Happer? When the Stars hit the locker room, they were trailing 8–5. And the momentum of their comeback was gone.

Josh took the blame onto himself. "You guys are playing fantastic. I just can't stop Happer. It's all my fault."

"No, it's mine," moaned Cal. "There's no reason for Oliver to beat me in the corners. I let everybody down."

"If I'd used my head for anything more than a hat rack," Alexia lamented in reverse volume control, "I would have thought of an aluminum stick three weeks ago. Then maybe we wouldn't have started the game in a five-goal hole."

What a *down* moment. I mean, getting blown out was bad enough. But to climb right back into this final only to watch it slip away — that had to be rock bottom. All the players chimed in with, "I should've skated faster," or "I should've checked harder" — "I should've this . . ." — "I should've that . . ." If I ever make it to *Sports Illustrated*, my first article is going to be called "There Are No Should'ves in Hockey."

Suddenly, Coach Bolitsky announced, "I have never been so proud of you as I am right now."

We were shocked — and it wasn't just because what he said was in perfect English. There stood the coach of the Stars, quivering with emotion.

That's when it hit me — Boom Boom Bolitsky didn't know anything about championships or winning or triumph. His whole NHL career was *this* — disappointment, frustration, trying to figure out what went wrong.

"I have nothing more to teach you," he continued with tears in his eyes. "You've become men." The praying-mantis gaze darted to Alexia. "And — you know — a doohickey."

What could we do? We hugged him. It just sort of happened. One minute we were all in our seats. The next, the whole team — Virgil included — was locked around the coach in a cross between an embrace and a football huddle. We were gross — the players were sweaty and wet with dirty snow, and I had a jacket covered in jalapeño-speckled cheese that was smearing on everybody else. But we didn't care. This just seemed so *right*.

The buzzer sounded, but the team hug didn't break up. Instead, we all kind of shuffled over to the exit. But we jammed up, so we had to kind of squeeze through. When the Penguins came from their own locker room, they found us oozing out the door like a giant swamp creature.

"You Martians are nuts" was Happer's opinion.

But that team hug turned out to be exactly what the Stars needed. They came out flying, rocking the Powerhouse Penguins back on their overconfident heels. If a stranger had wandered into the community center, he would have sworn that the team in green were the defending champs, and not the up-starts from the tiny town across the bridge. Trent was the first to score, completing his hat trick. Then Cal knocked in the rebound after one of Mike's shovel shots. Now it was 8–7.

Happer slowed down the steamrolling Stars by scoring on yet another wrist shot — his eighth goal in the two-game series. But the Stars came right back when Jared took a drop pass from Alexia and fired it between the goalie's legs.

9–8, Penguins. 1:12 remained on the clock.

Coach Bolitsky pulled Josh to give the Stars an extra attacker. Nail-biting time. The net was empty, yawning wide open like a cave. It was a huge target for the Penguins, who had so many great shooters — especially Happer.

But the defending champs ignored that open net like it wasn't even there. Instead, they dropped one defenseman back to protect the goalie. The other four formed a large moving square in the neutral zone, passing the puck back and forth between them.

"Last minute of play in the game," rumbled the PA announcement.

Boom Boom was the first to realize what was going on. "They're not going to shoot!" he bellowed. "They're just killing whatchamacallit!"

I checked the clock. 43 — 42 — 41 —

Brian dove to the ice, reaching out with his stick to intercept a pass. But it was just out of range.

"Hey, Martians!" jeered Happer, stickhandling. "You're running out of time!"

Suddenly, Alexia broke out of position and made a bull run right at him.

"No-o-o-o!" chorused Boom Boom and about half the Stars' fans, including me. She was leaving Happer a clear shot at our empty net.

But seeing the best checker in the league bearing down on him like a pouncing lion, Happer panicked and made a bad pass. It was intended for Oliver. But with a tremendous burst of speed that amazed even me, Trent sprang forward and snatched it up.

He had one man to beat. The move he put on the kid was almost impossible to describe except to say that he faked a fake. He began a classic deke to the backhand, then quickly pulled out of it and spun around the guy in the blink of an eye. The goalie was expecting another deke, so Trent shot early, snapping the puck a lot sooner than he had to.

"What are you *doing*?" I howled.

The Penguins' netminder had the fastest catcher in the league, and Trent knew it. The glove came up in perfect position to make the save. I watched in awe as the puck struck the bottom of the leather and dropped — *right into the net*!

Tie score — 9–9. I couldn't believe what lay ahead.

Sudden-death overtime.

Chapter 20 \ \ \ \ \

Boy, did I ever pick the wrong week to get kicked off the *Gazette*! I could write this up into the sports scoop of the century, but where would I publish it?

Right now, of course, my scoop was missing the most important part — the ending. Would it be the completion of the greatest underdog story since Cinderella herself? Or would the wicked stepsisters — the Penguins — prevail?

One thing was certain: I was reporting from memory alone from here on in, because all my tape machine could record was the roar of the crowd. People were up on their chairs, howling — even pregnant Mrs. B., who sprayed cracker crumbs as she cheered.

With the championship on the line, both teams started out cautious. But the action heated up fast.

The Stars had every reason to be confident. After all, they'd fought back from a 5–0 deficit today. There was only one problem.

"That rotten Happer," Mike said nervously. "Josh just can't seem to figure him out. If he gets a shot in overtime, we're cooked."

"Josh is a good goalie," I agreed, never taking my eyes from the ice. "But he's useless against that wrist shot. Not only can't he stop it — he always seems like he's jumping away from it!"

"Maybe it's a mental block," Cal suggested. "Like psychology. He can't make the save because he *thinks* he can't."

"He probably just guesses wrong," I mused sadly. "Either that or Happer looks one way and shoots the other."

I said it as a joke. But as it hung there in the air for a moment, the perfect truth of it struck every one of us. *That's* what Wayne Gretzky must have taught Happer — to use the direction of his eyes to get the goalie moving the wrong way. What else could turn an ordinary wrist shot into a deadly weapon?

"That's it!" we all chorused at the same time.

"That's what?" cried Boom Boom.

We filled him in on our theory about Happer's "magic" shot.

"We've got to tell Josh!" I finished. "Once he knows what to look for, he'll stop Happer every time!"

Coach Bolitsky got so excited that he leaped up on the bench. "Time-out!" he bawled.

"Forget it," the linesman shot back. "You've used your time-out."

And the play went raging on.

Boom Boom was not so easily discouraged. Reaching over the boards, he grabbed the nearest green sweater and pulled the player close to the bench. It was Virgil Knox.

"Get a whatchamacallit!" our coach hissed frantically.

"A whistle!" I shouted. "Stop the play! We've got to get a message to Josh!"

The little guy looked around. The action was all the way across the neutral zone. He would never get close enough to the puck to fall on it, freeze it, or golf it out of the rink.

I wanted to howl my frustration to the sky. We'd solved the mystery of Happer Feldman. But if Happer scored before we could get the message to Josh, it would all be for nothing.

Then our Virgil did the craziest, bravest, most brilliant thing. He squared his narrow shoulders, raised

136

the butt of his stick to his face mask, and skated full-tilt into the boards.

Crash! Bloodbath. Whistle.

Coach Bolitsky was appalled. He grabbed a handful of towels, vaulted onto the ice, and applied compresses to his injured player. "You ate wood on purpose!" he accused. "What did you do a stupid thingamajig like that for?"

I could just barely hear Virgil's smothered reply through the gusher. "Go tell Josh!" he urged. "Give him your message!"

Hearing this, Cal leaped over the boards and headed for the Stars' net. He and Josh held a long whispered conversation. When it was over, they were both looking directly at Happer. I distinctly heard Josh say "Got it!" He was grinning.

Much to Jared's disappointment, the referee refused to call out the Zamboni. They used towels to clean up the bloodstains, and overtime continued.

The face-off was in the Stars' end to Josh's left. Virgil had come to the bench to nurse his nose. So the Stars' lineup was Trent, Alexia, and Jared up front, with Brian and Kyle on defense — the same players who had taken the ice way back in October when the Stars from Mars had played their very first game.

Gavin jumped the gun on the face-off and was

waved out of the circle. Happer came in to take the draw against Trent.

"This is it, Ruben," growled Happer. "You and me."

Those two had been line mates and best friends up until this season. Now they were bitter rivals.

Trent won the face-off, but Happer hacked at his stick, sending the puck bouncing into the corner. Gavin chased after it with Alexia hot on his heels.

Wham! She sandwiched him between her shoulder and his own teammate, Oliver, who had come to help out. It was such a hard hit that both Penguins went down. The puck squirted loose, and, as Oliver fell, he swung his stick and golfed it out in front of the net.

And there, positioned where he always was, waited Happer Feldman — *all alone*!

"*No-o-o-o-o!*"

That wasn't only me; it was every Mars fan in the building.

He shot — that Wayne Gretzky wrist shot that had made him the leading scorer in the playoffs. And this time I could see his fake. His helmet — no, his entire body was focused on the *right* corner. Yet there was the puck, sizzling in on the *left*!

It was like the world ground to a halt. I saw the whole thing as a series of still pictures. The puck inched its way toward the net and a Penguins victory. Eight times before, Happer had taken this shot, and the result had been eight goals.

Then the still pictures began to change. I saw Josh, hurling himself across the crease. The puck was still headed for open net. At the last second, Josh flailed out with his stick and —

Thwack!

"He saved it!" I couldn't even hear myself over the roar of the crowd, but I knew I was howling because my throat was killing me.

The rebound rolled to Kyle, who began his backward rush.

Wham! Happer checked him from the side, and Kyle went down. But not before he passed off to Brian. Our speedster turned on the jets and blasted across the red line, leaving the Penguin forwards out of the play. When he head-manned the puck to Jared, the Stars had a three-on-two.

"Go-o-o-o-o!!"

One defenseman came up to challenge Jared, and our winger slipped the puck softly between the kid's skates through to Trent. With only one man back, our assistant captain decided against a deke. Instead, he accelerated, trying to beat the last defender with pure speed. And yeah, it worked. But when Trent came in on goal, he was at a sharp angle. A shot from there would miss for sure. But what choice did he have? He was almost at the red line.

Suddenly, he heard the sound of a stick banging the ice behind him — and not a wooden one either. In a lightning motion, he swung all the way around and backhanded the puck blindly out in front of the net.

The pass was way off target, but that didn't stop Alexia. She left her feet in a swan dive, flailing wildly at it with her stick.

Clink!

‖ ‖ ‖ *Chapter 21*

The tip of the aluminum blade caught just enough of the puck to flip it on its edge. An enormous gasp went up in the arena as it dribbled clear across the empty crease. Then, right when it was about to roll wide, it mysteriously changed direction, wobbled once, and flopped over into the net.

I know it sounds crazy, but for a split second, it didn't really sink in. It was like that for everybody. There was a shocked silence in the community center.

And then from Coach Bolitsky came a scream that I won't even attempt to describe. It wasn't celebration, or encouragement, or even happiness. It was just a release of pure energy. After sixteen disastrous years in the NHL, Boom Boom was finally a winner.

The Mars fans hit the roof. Some of them rushed

the ice, slipping, sliding, and dancing with glee. The rest stayed at rinkside, pounding on the glass and cheering.

As for the Stars themselves, *Insanity!* was too tame a headline for this moment. They were bringing one another down with flying tackles as they struggled to pile onto Alexia, the goal scorer. I was out there with them, wrestling, hugging, leaping, and howling. It was better than just a *Sports Illustrated* moment. It was a hundred great stories all rolled up into one — a Cinderella team, a spectacular comeback, justice triumphing over unfairness, and outsiders finally earning their rightful place. It was a championship, but it was so much more. It was high voltage, mega-powered, H-bomb, supernova, fantastic!

Our two captains, Alexia and Trent, who'd spent half the season fighting, were bonking their helmets together and laughing with sheer joy. It was that pair that finally dug out the championship-winning puck and presented it to our beloved coach.

He took it and passed it on to the Star who deserved it more than any other. Was it Alexia, who scored the winning goal? Or Trent or Jared, who assisted on it? Was it Josh, who made the big save? No.

"Virgil," said Boom Boom to his newest player, "if

you didn't eat wood to get us that whistle, we probably would have lost this thingamabob. You're the toughest little whosis I've ever seen, and I think you should have this dingus."

A faint look of hope found its way onto Virgil's mousy features. "You mean you don't hate me anymore?"

Our laughter was interrupted by oohs and aahs. Mr. Feldman was approaching, carrying the Feldman Cup. Let me tell you, the silver trophy had never gleamed as brightly as it did that day under the lights of the community center.

Alexia looked around gleefully. "Where's my buddy Happer? I want to make sure he gets a good look at us laying our alien fingers on his precious cup."

"Fingers?" chortled Josh. "I'm going to do a lot more than just touch it! I'm going to hug it and kiss it and maybe even marry it!"

"Boom Boom," came Mrs. Bolitsky's voice from behind us. "It's time."

"Yeah, I know!" crowed the coach. "They're going to give us the Feldman heejazz!"

"No, no," she insisted. "I mean it's *time*! The baby's coming!"

Shocked, he turned to face her. "But — but — the baby isn't due until June!"

"Well, tell that to the baby!" she said crossly. "It's coming! We've got to get to the hospital!"

In a panic, Boom Boom ran over and tried to guide her through the crowd to the nearest exit. They didn't make an inch of progress. People were jammed at rinkside twenty deep. Between the wildly celebrating Marsers and the Penguins fans trying to leave, there was absolute, total gridlock.

The coach turned to try for the south exit. It was even more crowded that way. He looked really worried. "How are we ever going to get out of this doojig?"

And suddenly, there was a roar of heavy machinery, and a voice called, "Coach — over here!"

We all gawked. Partying spectators were scattering out of the way as the Zamboni roared across the ice. There at the wheel sat Jared Enoch.

The praying-mantis eyes bulged. "Jared!" cried Boom Boom. "What the heck do you think you're doing?"

Jared pointed to the open Zamboni gate in the boards. It led to a special exit to the parking lot where the ice scrapings were dumped. "I can get you out of here, Coach!" he promised. "Hop on!"

Now, we were all pretty much used to Jared and his harebrained ideas. And using a Zamboni driven by a twelve-year-old as an ambulance ranks right up there with the all-time classics.

On the other hand, what choice did the coach have? The exits were blocked. And having the baby in a hockey rink wasn't an option. He led his wife out onto the ice and lifted her up to the running board of the big machine. As he climbed on himself, he wagged a finger at Jared. "Drive whatchamacal-lit!"

"Carefully," translated Mrs. B. faintly.

"Jared!" cried Cal. "Where are you going?"

"The hospital!" Jared called back, stepping on the gas and wheeling a perfect one-eighty on the ice.

Alexia leaped onto a bumper. "No way is this baby going to get born without me!"

"And me!" added Trent, jumping on beside her.

Every single Star, including the team ex-reporter, crammed onto that Zamboni. You should have seen it. A bunch of guys were piled onto the hood, trying not to slide off the sides. Mike lay flat at Jared's feet. Virgil had his stick wrapped around the back of the driver's seat and was holding on for dear life, eyes tightly shut. As for Jared — well, this was his finest hour. He'd driven this thing so many times in his dreams that he was an old pro.

Mr. Feldman was galloping beside us, howling

like a madman. "Come back here with my Zamboni!"

"Sorry, Mr. Feldman!" bellowed Jared. "We've got an appointment at the maternity ward!"

And we were out of the building and into the parking lot.

The hospital was right down the street from the community center. Jared piloted the Zamboni along the sidewalk.

"Get out of the way!" he hollered at some poor man out walking his dog. "Championship hockey team with pregnant lady coming through!"

We pulled up right under the sign that said EMERGENCY. They probably weren't used to a lot of patients arriving by Zamboni, but they were pretty nice about it. They whisked the coach and his wife into Maternity and directed the rest of us to the waiting room. I don't think they were too thrilled with the team's skates cutting up their linoleum. And they made everybody put their sticks in the umbrella stand.

We settled in to wait for news.

"You know," I said, "Happer Feldman was right all along. None of us Marsers ever did touch the cup. We left just before they could present it to us."

"Don't worry," soothed Trent. "We'll get our trophy. They can't keep it from us just because we had a medical emergency." He looked nervous. "I hope Mrs. B. and the baby are okay."

"What's the big delay?" complained Cal. "We've been here ten minutes already. How long does it take to have a baby?"

"My mom says it took twenty-two hours to have me," ventured Fragile.

"Twenty-two hours?" cried Jared. "Oh, man, I should have put more quarters in the parking meter!"

Actually, the news came pretty quickly. Boom Boom walked into the room. We all jumped to our feet. This was the big moment.

"It's whatchamacallit," he announced.

There was silence as we drank this in.

Alexia spoke first. "Yeah, but is it a boy whatchamacallit or a girl whatchamacallit?"

"No, it's *whatchamacallit*!" the coach insisted.

Mrs. B. appeared behind him, still big as a house. "It's indigestion," she translated sheepishly. "Too many jalapeños. It was a false alarm."

And by the time we got back to the community center to claim our trophy, everybody was gone.

Chapter 22 \ \ \ \ \ \

"So, Clarence," said Dr. Mendez, "I hear your Stars won the championship yesterday. Tell me all about it."

Didn't it figure? The one guy in all of Waterloo who wasn't ignoring the Stars' big win like it never happened, and I had fourteen pounds of dentist's equipment jammed into my mouth. I couldn't have managed a grunt, let alone a play-by-play description of the greatest Cinderella story in the history of hockey.

Still, I had no complaints about my early Monday morning appointment. I had only two cavities — way better than the eleven I'd racked up last time. I was drilled and filled and walking into school before the nine o'clock bell. My destination: the cafeteria, and a certain star map of the Milky Way that just so happened to be made out of jawbreakers. I didn't have another checkup for six whole months, and I was planning to celebrate by eating half the galaxy, clear through to the Big Dipper — most of it before lunch. I was going to re-earn my nickname, Chipmunk. After today, they might even have to call me Blowfish.

I ran into the Stars gathered around the main display case outside the office. There, padlocked behind thick glass, gleamed the Feldman Cup.

"Can you believe that rotten Mr. Feldman?" exclaimed Josh in disgust. "He's fixed it so we can't have our trophy."

"He's just mad because the police impounded the Zamboni," put in Jared. "How was I supposed to know I was parked in a tow-away zone?"

"You could have read the sign," offered Alexia. "It said, 'Tow-Away Zone.'"

"Hey," said Jared, irritated. "It was my first time driving, and I think I did a pretty good job."

"We didn't get a baby," Cal pointed out.

"You can't blame that on me!" Jared exploded. "Even a real NHL Zamboni driver couldn't have gotten a baby!"

"That lousy Happer is still right," I said wistfully. "We'll never lay a finger on that trophy now."

"Not unless somebody brought a brick," agreed Alexia.

"Don't let it get to you," Trent soothed. "They present it to us again — at the June sports banquet. And then we'll have our team name engraved on it."

By the time I got to the cafeteria, Mr. Lambert had already started the morning announcements.

". . . and in the Slapshot League finals yesterday, the Powerhouse Penguins played a great series, but came up just short, losing 10–9."

I wasn't even surprised. Leave it to those Waterloo types to rave about their precious Penguins even when they lose, and never think to mention who beat them. What about "Congratulations, Stars, for winning the championship in your very first season?" Fat chance. I'll bet Mr. Lambert wasn't even being mean. It just never crossed his mind to talk about a team that wasn't from Waterloo.

I bypassed the food line and went straight to the skylit spot where my "science project" was hanging. My gasp made everybody turn around. I'm pretty sure it sucked in half the air in the room.

My big blue blanket and all Mrs. B.'s hundreds of jawbreakers were gone!

Mrs. Spiro came up to me. "Good morning, Clarence. I suppose you're wondering what happened to your science project."

"Somebody ate it!" I wailed.

She laughed. "Oh, you're such a jokester. Mr. Ping

was so impressed by your work that he entered it in the North American Science Fair in Anchorage, Alaska."

"Alaska," I repeated, stunned. "That's far." I brightened. "But science fairs only last a few days, right? My — uh — galaxy will be coming back soon."

"Oh, no," she said seriously. "After the fair, all the projects are going on tour to schools across the continent for the next five and a half months. Isn't it exciting?"

"I can't get over it," I mumbled. I wouldn't see my jawbreakers again until two weeks before my next dentist appointment, when I didn't dare eat them!

Mrs. Spiro looked me in the eye. "Clarence, I really admire your behavior these last couple of weeks. When I had to remove you from the paper, you could have sulked and developed a bad attitude. Instead, you focused your energy on something positive and handed in a science project that obviously took a lot of effort and creativity."

I pictured myself frantically bundling up those jawbreakers in my blue blanket and heaving them out the window so my mom wouldn't find them.

"I don't believe in shortcuts," I agreed wearily. "I do everything the hard way."

"Well, I think you've earned another chance," she said. "Come back and work with me on the *Gazette*."

My heart soared. Chipmunk Adelman was a reporter again! Now no one would be able to ignore the Cinderella story of the Stars from Mars. It would all be laid out in my column in the Gazette.

Look out, *Sports Illustrated*! Here I come!

The June sports banquet was the biggest event of the year in Waterloo junior athletics. The fried chicken dinner featured the official trophy presentation for everything from kindergarten T-ball to high school cheerleading. Somewhere in there, the Stars were due to get the Feldman Cup.

They made us wait. Oh, man, did they make us wait! They gave away every Girl Scout badge and Wiffle-ball ribbon before they got to us. There we sat at our table in the back corner of the community center meeting hall, so far from the stage that the other winners looked like ants. Sure, it was a pretty big dis. But we were having a party back there, toasting our championship with soda and piling up chicken bones. The players were all waggling their index fingers at one another. These were the alien fingers that they were all going to lay on the Feldman Cup, just to stick it to Happer. Those Waterloo types could ignore us and give us the worst seats in the house. But they couldn't change the fact that we'd won.

I'll bet we ate and drank more than any other table

there. Of course, that was mostly because we had Mrs. Bolitsky. Remember in April when I said she couldn't get any bigger? Well, she got bigger. The coach's wife was the size of three people.

After two pretty boring hours, our moment finally came. Mr. Feldman stood up there with a phony smile plastered on his face.

"Now it's time to present the Feldman Cup to the Slapshot League champions, the Stars."

The applause was polite — not exactly the standing ovation the Penguins got every year, but it still felt good. I ran ahead of the players, then wheeled and backed up, snapping pictures of the team and their coach as they went to accept their prize. The last *Gazette* of the school year was due out next week, and I was planning to do a photo spread so big that *Sports Illustrated* would be jealous. I even had a headline for it, maybe my best ever: *Cup Crazy*.

Because the applause was kind of quiet, we were able to hear her clearly.

"Boom Boom, it's time."

"Yeah," called Josh gleefully. "We're finally getting our trophy!"

The players were so intent on walking up there that they didn't notice the coach had stopped in his tracks, frozen like a statue.

She said it again. "Boom Boom, it's time. The baby's coming."

The whole team just shifted into reverse. We collected Mrs. B. and headed for the door, leaving Mr. Feldman up there with his mouth hanging open and nobody to receive his trophy.

Jared started for the arena. "I'll get the Zamboni!"

"Oh, no thanks," Mrs. B. said quickly. "We'll take the van."

So there we were again, the whole team and me, sitting in the maternity waiting room — and not just for a few minutes this time.

We got restless. We paced. We cleaned out the candy machine. Mostly, we talked about the Feldman Cup. No matter how hard we tried, what Happer said was coming true. We were never going to get to touch it.

"'Happer said, Happer said,'" mimicked Alexia in reverse volume control. "Happer has said enough for one lifetime."

"A trophy is just a thing," Fragile said philosophically. "Whether we get it or not, we still won." Sometimes it takes a clueless guy to cut right to the heart of the matter.

Suddenly, Coach Bolitsky burst through the doorway, looking like he'd just stuck his finger in an electric socket.

"It's whatchamacallit!" he blurted.

"Aw, not again," groaned Cal. "I told her she was eating too much coleslaw."

"No!" cried Boom Boom. "It's a whatsit! A whosis! A *boy*!"

We cheered quietly because the nurse was watching. But in spirit, we were screaming our lungs out. The littlest Star had hit the ice.

"How's Mrs. B.?" Alexia asked.

"First class," said the new dad. "She needs to rest now. But I can take you in to see baby whatsisname."

So we all trooped down to the nursery and pressed our noses up against the glass. There he was, a really tiny guy, wrapped in a blue blanket. He was wrinkled and bald and toothless, so you could see the family resemblance on the father's side. But he was cute anyway. Hopefully, he would grow up to look more like his mom.

A cardboard sign on the crib proclaimed: CLETUS BOLITSKY JR.

"*Cletus?!*" It came from half the team.

"That's me," confirmed the coach. "Boom Boom is just my nickname from when I played in the doohickey."

I watched as the newborn gave a big yawn and re-settled himself in his crib.

Someday, I thought, when he gets older, I'm going

to tell Cletus Jr. about his mom and dad and the amazing Cinderella miracle season of the Stars from Mars. He won't believe me. Who would? But I'll tell him anyway.

That's what reporters do.

About the Author

"I've always been a sports nut," says Gordon Korman. "And growing up in Montreal and Toronto, hockey was the biggest game in town. My mother insists that I was named after Detroit Red Wings legend Gordie Howe, who was her favorite player when she was a teenager."

Gordon Korman has written more than twenty books for middle-grade and young adult readers, among them *Liar, Liar, Pants on Fire; The Chicken Doesn't Skate; Why Did the Underwear Cross the Road?; The Toilet Paper Tigers;* and seven books in the popular Bruno and Boots series, all published by Scholastic. He lives with his wife and son in Long Island, New York.